"Am I being kidnapped?"

Felice shot Tobias an apologetic look. "Do you mind? I promise it's only temporary."

"If it's my body you're after, you'd better let me arrange the time and place," Tobias drawled. "The spirit's willing but the car's inadequate. We're both too big."

Felice smothered a laugh. "That wasn't why I kidnapped you. I just wanted to show you Woodlands."

"Well, that's shot me down. You know, I thought I'd been warned about all the hazards of my inheritance but—" his eyes swept deliberately over her "—I think the most obvious hazard was missed out. Nobody said anything about beautiful blond Amazons."

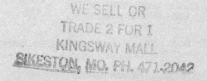

Anne Beaumont started out as a Jill-of-all-writing-trades, but she says it was her experience as a magazine fiction editor, buying stories and condensing them for serialization, that taught her to separate the bones of a story from the flesh. In her own writing, she starts with her characters—"a heroine I can identify with, then a hero who seems right for her." She says that many writers work in reverse—plot first, then characters. "That's fine," she says. "If we all had the same method, we might all be writing the same books, and what a crashing bore that would be!" In addition to Anne Beaumont's romance novels, the author has written historicals under the pen name Rosina Pyatt. She lives on the Isle of Wight, with its sparkling white beaches, and has three children, of whom she is immensely proud.

Books by Anne Beaumont

HARLEQUIN ROMANCE

3049—ANOTHER TIME, ANOTHER LOVE
3199—A CINDERELLA AFFAIR
3241—IMAGES OF DESIRE

HARLEQUIN PRESENTS

1231—THAT SPECIAL TOUCH
1391—SECRET WHISPERS

FEELINGS OF LOVE
Anne Beaumont

Harlequin Books

TORONTO • NEW YORK • LONDON
AMSTERDAM • PARIS • SYDNEY • HAMBURG
STOCKHOLM • ATHENS • TOKYO • MILAN
MADRID • WARSAW • BUDAPEST • AUCKLAND

Original hardcover edition published in 1992
by Mills & Boon Limited

ISBN 0-373-17139-0

Harlequin Romance first edition June 1993

FEELINGS OF LOVE

CHAPTER ONE

FELICE LAWSON snuggled deeper into her pillows, the phone held more or less against her ear, her eyes refusing to open. Huskily she grumbled, 'Jack, at seven o'clock on a Sunday morning my sense of humour's a bit thin. This is a joke, isn't it?'

She knew it was a useless protest, that it wasn't any joke. Jack Carter didn't have a sense of humour. He did have a bit of a conscience, though, because he apologised, 'Sorry, Felice. I wouldn't call you out like this if it wasn't urgent. Dave was on his way to make the pick-up when his clutch went, and the job is in your neck of the woods.'

'Nothing is in my neck of the woods. You're the one who's always moaning that I live at the back of beyond,' she pointed out, but she knew she was only stalling for time—time to get her eyes open and her head up off the pillow. She needed the extra money she earned as a weekend taxi driver.

Jack knew that, but he also knew she hadn't finished ferrying home the last of the Saturday night disco revellers until just over four hours ago.

'This customer is bound for Woodlands Hall, and that's practically on your doorstep. You can't miss it, it's the only thing that is,' Jack came back at her, sarcasm filtering through his wheedling tone.

Woodlands Hall! Felice sat up, her curiosity getting the better of her sleepiness. 'There must be a mistake,' she replied. 'The Hall's empty. It's been locked up for

months. It looks like something out of an Agatha
Christie novel, all creepy and shuttered and overgrown.
Nobody in their right mind would want to go there,
specially first thing on a Sunday morning. I reckon somebody's playing a practical joke on you, Jack.'

That was all right with her, but not when the joke
stretched to her losing sleep. She snuggled down again
and yawned. It wasn't unknown for somebody to get a
kick out of sending taxis out on hoax calls. 'Have you
upset anybody lately?' she went on, her voice getting
huskier as sleep fought to reclaim her.

'No, I haven't,' Jack replied, incensed, 'and this is a
genuine booking. It was phoned through from London
yesterday. I'd cover for Dave myself but I'm on the other
side of the island and I can't get there in time.'

'Where's "there"?' Felice asked, sighing fatalistically
as she sat up again. Even if it was a hoax, she would
have to turn out. It was a nuisance, but it was no use
fighting it any longer. Jack definitely had a bee in his
bonnet about this one.

'Woodlands Airfield, not even ten minutes from you.
A chap called Tobias Hunter is flying himself in
and——'

'Who?' Felice exclaimed, the name working on her
like a charm. She flung aside the continental quilt and
swung her long legs out of bed.

'Tobias Hunter,' Jack repeated, sounding perplexed.
'He's due in——' there was a pause as he consulted his
watch '—fifteen minutes. It would have been twenty if
you hadn't argued so much. If he wants to play spooks
at the Hall that's up to him. Just pick him up from the
airfield and get him there.'

'I'm on my way.' Felice slammed down the receiver
and began rushing around like a soul possessed. For a

big girl, she was surprisingly swift and graceful, even when propelled by excitement.

So the mystery man had surfaced at last! Nearly six months of nail-biting anxiety waiting to learn whether he even existed, and he had to pick dawn on a freezing February morning to prove that he did.

Wide awake now, she forgave him. She had every reason to. Never before had she been so anxious to meet a man, and providence in the guise of a broken clutch had given her the perfect opportunity. What was more, she'd have him all to herself. She wouldn't waste a minute of it.

In record time Felice was in her car and zooming along the winding road that cut through the beech wood as fast as the frosty surface would permit. She glanced at the overgrown driveway to the Hall as she passed it, noting that the ornate iron gates were still firmly padlocked. They'd been that way ever since old Joshua Hunter had died, an embittered eccentric to the last.

She wondered whether this unknown Tobias Hunter was anything like him. Surely not! Old Josh had to be a one-off! In fact, nobody had known he'd had any relatives until he'd died without leaving a will and a search for an heir had been instigated.

Record of a brother, long since dead, had been discovered, then of a nephew, also dead. The last Felice had heard, the search had switched to Canada to discover whether a great-nephew, Tobias, was still alive.

Apparently he was, and very much so if he was hearty enough to fly himself in on a morning like this, Felice mused, as the car dipped into the gentle slope of the valley where the airfield was sited.

It was on Hunter land, although it was leased out to an aviation company, but the fact that it existed might encourage the last of the Hunters to stay. It would be nice for a man who could fly to have an airstrip in his own back yard.

It was very much in Felice's interests that Tobias Hunter settle on the island. The last thing she wanted was for him to take one look at his inheritance then sell up and go away. If that was what he intended, she would do her very best to change his mind, even if she hated him on sight.

Reason told her, though, that he couldn't possibly be as crusty to deal with as Old Josh. Nobody could.

She craned her head around and listened for the sound of a plane as she approached the airfield, but there was nothing. Damn, he must be down already. If he was unfortunate enough to have inherited any of Old Josh's genes he wouldn't appreciate being kept waiting for his taxi. She'd so much wanted to make a good impression, too!

Felice wished she'd got out of bed as soon as Jack had phoned instead of giving him such a hard time, but how was she to know the lost heir was on his way to look over Woodlands? She didn't have a crystal ball, even if her eyes had been open enough to look into one.

She drove on to the airfield, stopped by the small hangar and studied three little planes parked neatly away from the landing strip. There was enough frost on them to show they'd been there all night.

There was no sign of a new arrival, no sign of any life at all. Normally she wouldn't expect any. For one thing it was a Sunday, and for another not much commercial use was made of the airfield until the holidaymakers' joy flights started in the summer season.

Felice looked at her watch. It was twenty minutes since she'd taken Jack's call. She wondered again if this was a hoax, and yet the name Tobias Hunter was authentic enough. It had certainly got her here in double-quick time.

She got out of the car, closed the door and leaned against it, looking up at the sky. She was a vibrant, glowing figure in the grey, winter-bare landscape. She seemed to have the knack of storing summer and always carrying a breath of it with her, no matter what the season.

Her hastily scrubbed face was rosy and her thick hair, scuffed back into a ponytail, was the colour of corn bleached under a blazing sun. Her eyes were the blue of an unclouded August sky, and they were made all the more brilliant by the long dark lashes fringing them. Her teeth were white and gleaming, and her complexion was never pasty. Summer or winter, she was always bonny.

The burden Felice had to bear, as far as she was concerned anyway, was her size. She stood five feet ten inches in her flat-heeled knee-length boots and, although her waist was neat, her voluptuous curves definitely flowed on the generous side.

Yearning, in those rare moments when she had the time to yearn, to be a willowy beauty like Janetta, her younger sister, or Serena, her top-model cousin, she had to settle for being a sturdy Amazon. It was the joker in an otherwise perfect pack.

Men were fascinated by Janetta and Serena, content to worship them from afar if they couldn't get any closer. Felice they grappled, treating her as if she were some kind of all-in wrestler who might get the better of them if they handled her with care.

At twenty-six, Felice was used to it. That didn't make it any better, but she'd learned to be philosophical. She'd long since stopped looking for a man who'd place her on a pedestal alongside her female relations, and she supposed it was just as well.

For a start, it would have to be a pretty solid pedestal, and she'd probably be bored to tears up there, anyway. As she looked so capable, everybody always assumed that she was, and from being a young child she'd done all her own lifting and carrying, worrying and managing. No wonder she'd grown up on the bossy side.

It was too late in the day to learn the tricks Janetta and Serena had been born knowing. Anyway, the sad fact was that neither nature nor fate had fashioned her into a coquette. She'd simply never had the time or chance to practise.

And she'd sort of got used to men treating her, after the inevitable wrestling match, more like one of the boys than a prospective bride.

She didn't suppose this Tobias Hunter would be any different, either. If she fluttered her long eyelashes at him, he'd probably ask if she had something in her eye.

Oh, well, Felice thought, ever practical, at least it was easier to deal with men once they understood there wasn't going to be any sex involved. Besides, this Tobias Hunter might be married. She found herself hoping that he was.

The Isle of Wight, separated eons ago from mainland England by a thin strip of water, was a perfect place to bring up children, especially in a spot as rural and beautiful as Woodlands Hall.

Yes, it could definitely help if there were little Hunters running around.

Felice, her curvy thighs encased in faded blue jeans and her page-two bosom hidden under a fur-lined leather jacket, turned up her collar as the frost-edged wind began to chill her face. She thrust her hands deep into her pockets then cocked her head as the faint drone of an engine gently overlaid the early morning silence.

She shivered, but it was nothing to do with the cold. It was pure excitement. So much depended on what sort of a man Tobias Hunter turned out to be. She pictured him as a younger version of Old Josh, with steely grey eyes, a hooked nose and shoulders as wide as he was high.

In a word, formidable.

Just as well she wasn't easily intimidated, Felice reflected ruefully, as the sound of an engine solidified into a plane circling over the sea to come in. Sometimes it was useful to be big enough to intimidate men.

Felice watched critically as the light plane, buffeted by the gusty wind, lost height and lined up for the runway. In these weather conditions a lesser man would have settled for the train and ferry, and she felt a gleam of admiration for the unknown Tobias.

It seemed he was the type who, having made up his mind about something, wasn't easily put off. If she'd been younger and not set so rigidly in the practical mould nature had made for her, she might have thought he was a man after her own heart.

It was a good thing she was philosophical instead of romantic, she mused, otherwise she might be feeling wistful. A man after her own heart indeed! As if she didn't know that all they were ever after was her body.

Did she feel wistful, anyway? Felice sighed and tried to convince herself she didn't.

She found herself holding her breath as the little plane swooped over the trees, seeming to falter as it fought the wind. She could imagine the tussle that was going on at the controls to keep it on course. It cleared the trees and the high hedge enclosing the runway then flopped down like a tired bird that had flown too long.

Felice sighed with relief as the plane turned and taxied to the only windbreak the airfield offered, the lee of the hangar where the other planes were parked. The engine cut, there was a pause, and then she straightened up as a man emerged.

Her future, and that of her family, was riding on what sort of a man Tobias Hunter proved to be. Surprise was her first reaction. This man was big. He had the height to balance the shoulder-width she expected of a Hunter, having only Old Josh to go on.

He didn't hesitate or waste time looking around him but came straight towards her, and she got a distinct impression of determination, of a purpose that wasn't easily thwarted.

Felice felt a swift surge of illicit excitement and suppressed it just as swiftly. She didn't want him to be so positively male—not if it made her react in such a positively female way! She hadn't allowed for that, and as she studied him more closely her eyes widened. There were other things about him she hadn't allowed for, either.

He's a good six inches taller than me, she thought, and it took her a few moments to come to terms with that because she'd towered over Old Josh. This Hunter, it seemed, had broken the mould. His shoulders were broad, all right, but he looked perfectly proportioned. His hips were slim and he moved lithely, his long legs cutting the distance between them in no time at all.

He was dressed pretty much as she was, in jeans and a fur-lined leather jacket, and the only thing that was out of place in this rural setting was the leather briefcase that swung from his left hand. His other hand was

pushing back a lock of unruly black hair that the wind
was tumbling about his forehead.

Somewhere on the other side of thirty, she guessed.
An interesting age...

Felice had just a few seconds more to concentrate on
his face, and she made full use of them. Not a handsome
man, she thought, as she took in his craggy features,
then immediately wondered if that impression was fair.
With a strong nose, chiselled cheekbones and chin, firm
lips and a scar or two, his was definitely a man's face.
It had its own power to attract—or would have done,
she corrected herself hastily, if she'd been a romantic.

Besides, only seconds ago she'd realised it wouldn't
do for sexual overtones to clutter up her relationship with
Tobias Hunter. And, since she'd already managed to
survive for twenty-six years without allowing sex to side-
track her from what was really important, she wasn't
about to fall apart now.

Silently applauding her own good sense, Felice told
herself that if she'd felt a momentary weakness it was
only because this man was so different from what she'd
expected. After all, she was an assertive, capable woman.
It was the helpless ones who were vulnerable to first
impressions. If anybody was going to be overpowered
here, it was likely to be Tobias Hunter.

Like it or not, it was the effect she had on men, and
she couldn't see this encounter on a freezing February
morning making any difference.

Did she feel a twinge of regret about that?

No, Felice told herself sternly, and forced herself to
think about the wife and children she wanted to move
into Woodlands Hall. This man couldn't possibly be a
bachelor—not looking the way he did and sending out

sexual signals that even she could pick up. When her mind was on other things, too! Or supposed to be.

Her moment of weakness past, and very much herself again, Felice seized the initiative as a matter of course. Tobias Hunter had stopped just one pace away and she held out her hand, saying, 'Felice Lawson.'

All right, so taxi drivers didn't usually introduce themselves, but she wasn't the usual sort of taxi driver and it never occurred to her to meet anybody on less than an equal footing, even Tobias Hunter. They were going to be neighbours.

If all went well...

To give him his due, he looked more amused than affronted. He took her hand, and said, 'Tobias Hunter. I wasn't expecting a female driver.'

Felice would have preferred 'lady' to 'female' but she smiled, and she had a smile that wasn't easily forgotten. It started in her eyes, lifted her lips and brought an added glow to her face. 'Most people don't, but you can relax. I guarantee not to wrap you around a tree,' she replied easily, used to men making a thing out of her driving a taxi.

'What else do you guarantee?' he asked, a pleasant hint of a drawl in his deep voice.

She liked his voice but was startled by his question. This wasn't the usual reply she got to her working patter—and he was still holding her hand. His grip was firm and strong. His warmth transmitted itself to her gloveless fingers and, she thought a trifle breathlessly, something of his strength was transmitted as well. It was a nice feeling.

She realised then that, whatever effect she was having on him, she wasn't overpowering him. Respect dawned.

She didn't quite know where they were going from here, but respect was a pretty good place to start.

'You're not afraid of me,' she said impulsively. 'Most men are. They take one look at me and feel their manhood threatened.'

'My manhood's more secure than that,' he replied, answering her smile with a knockout of his own, 'and I'm still waiting for an answer to my question.'

Felice chuckled. It was a novelty to meet a man who wasn't easily side-tracked. She drew her fingers out of his but the warmth remained. She knew why. She liked him, and the feeling that she'd met a friend was spreading the warmth pleasantly through her entire body. It was something separate from sexual attraction, something she valued.

'Do I have to guarantee anything else? Most men, when confronted with a lady driver, are happy to settle for a safe arrival.'

'You'll have to stop confusing me with other men,' he replied, his eyes teasing hers. They were grey, but not steely like Old Josh's. They were darker, warmer, more intimate...

Felice felt breathless again, and gave herself another scold to scotch the wild idea that he was flirting with her. This man was a Canadian. Naturally he'd be less formal than the Englishmen she was used to, and consequently more friendly. She could scarcely pick nits about that. After all, she'd given him the lead.

She'd wanted Tobias Hunter to be a friend. It had just happened a lot sooner than she'd expected, that's all. She should count that a plus and stop making these unnecessary emotional waves.

She was congratulating herself on getting her head together when she noticed he was watching the play of emotions across her face with a slight smile on his lips. She had the awful feeling he'd been reading her mind, and very nearly blushed.

'Can I take it you won't confuse me with anybody else again?' he asked, his voice strangely challenging.

Felice almost felt cross. Tobias Hunter was seizing the initiative at every turn, and just as shamelessly as she normally seized it herself. It was another novel feeling, having the tables turned on her, but it didn't do her respect for him any harm. She gave him a thoughtful look, and replied, 'I think I'm getting your measure now.'

'Good. I think I'm getting yours.'

What am I supposed to make of that? Felice wondered. Then she told herself she was being ridiculously sensitive, and she laughed.

'I like that,' he said.

'What?'

'The way you laugh.'

Damn, he'd done it again. Knocked her sideways by saying the unexpected. She recovered quickly and quipped, 'It beats crying.'

It was his turn to laugh, and she liked the way he laughed, too. She realised she was beginning to enjoy herself, perhaps because she'd always enjoyed a challenge—and Tobias was definitely a challenge. Again she felt a swift rush of warmth towards him. It was so long since she'd met anybody to stimulate her, to laugh with. It was almost as if he were a kindred soul.

Her delight was mirrored in her eyes as she said, 'I'm glad you're amused, because I doubt if you will be when you get to the Hall. It's been shut up since Old Josh died. I hope somebody warned you about that.'

'I thought I'd been warned about all the hazards of my inheritance but——' his eyes swept deliberately from her golden head to her size nine boots '—I think the most obvious hazard was missed out. Nobody said anything about Amazonian blondes.'

Felice's eyes sparkled with a mixture of indignation and amusement. 'Thanks very much! I'm not part of the Hunter inheritance.'

'I didn't expect everything to be perfect,' he replied smoothly.

'You're not likely to be disappointed, then,' she retorted, determined he wasn't going to fluster her again.

Tobias just smiled and opened the car door for her, a courtesy she didn't expect, since he was the customer. She was touched, though, and so she had to joke, 'Are you sure you wouldn't like to drive as well?'

'Don't you trust your driving?'

'Of course I do!' she exclaimed.

'Then so will I.'

Felice stared after him as he closed her door and walked around the car, wondering if she really had his measure, after all. He attacked—then disarmed—with a very potent blend of challenge and charm. No wonder she was having such a hard time discovering whether she was on her head or her heels.

More to the point, he was earning all the Brownie points and she had to win some back. It wasn't at all like her to be so dozy. She leaned across and opened the other front door. 'Why don't you sit beside me?' she suggested quickly. 'We're very friendly down here.'

'I've noticed,' he murmured as he got in beside her, and immediately her roomy saloon seemed to shrink. He was a big man, all right.

Felice gave him a sidelong look as she started the engine. She was trying to judge whether their friendship had developed enough for her to presume on it. Her blue eyes met his grey, and it was hers that broke the contact. Better wait a while, she decided, and smothered a sigh as she swung the car out on to the road. Patience wasn't her strong point.

'Say it,' he prompted.

'What?'

'Whatever you nearly bit your tongue off not to say.'

She was startled into taking a bend too fast, fought to hold the car steady as the wheels skidded on the frosty surface, and muttered under her breath as she regained control.

'You can say that, too, if you like,' he offered.

Felice began to laugh again. There were certain things she wanted from this man, very important things, but she was having trouble concentrating on them. Tobias kept turning the tables on her, beguiling her into behaving as though this were some kind of outing. Somehow he made her feel frivolous, light-headed—and feminine.

It was the feminine bit that worried her the most.

'Mr Hunter——' she began, ignoring the road that led to the Hall and nosing the car into a high-hedged lane that led upwards to the cliffs.

'Tobias,' he interrupted.

Felice nodded in unconscious agreement. Of course it was Tobias. From the word go there'd been no formality between them, so it would be ridiculous to start now. 'Tobias,' she began again, and stopped.

'Yes?'

'I like you,' she said, and then really could have bitten off her tongue. Curse her impulsiveness! That wasn't what she'd meant to say at all...

CHAPTER TWO

WHAT an idiot he must think her, and what an idiot she felt! How could she have blurted out anything so inane? He must think she was chatting him up and she wasn't! At least, not in the you-man-me-woman sense. All right, so he'd had a certain physical impact on her, but she was over that now. They were friends, and that was the most important thing.

Felice thought of the wife that must be somewhere in the background, and the little Hunters, and almost died of embarrassment. She said quickly, 'I didn't mean that the way it sounded.'

'Don't disappoint me now,' he replied. 'I was just about to say I like you, too.'

Felice felt relief whoosh through her and said eagerly, 'You mean in a friendly sort of way?' She didn't wait for an answer but rushed on, 'That's what I meant, too. I'm just so pleased you're nothing like your great-uncle that my enthusiasm ran away with me.'

'That's shot me down in flames,' Tobias replied.

The last of Felice's embarrassment vanished and she chuckled. 'Who are you kidding? It would take more than me to shoot you down. When we went into a skid back there you didn't turn a hair. You didn't even remind me I'd guaranteed not to wrap you around a tree. Most men would have...when they'd stopped screaming!'

'But we've already agreed I'm not like most men,' he pointed out.

No, you're not, she silently agreed. Like Old Josh, you're a one-off, but in a much more attractive way. She was wondering how to put that into words without sounding flirty when he said, 'Do you know your meter isn't running?'

'Yes, I know,' she replied, grateful for the change of subject. 'This part of the ride is a diversion. My idea, so there's no charge.' She bit her lip as she wondered how he would take that. A new friendship was a fragile thing. She could be guilty of pushing it too far.

'Am I being kidnapped?'

Felice shot him an apologetic look. 'Do you mind? I promise it's only temporary.'

'Somebody should have warned me that life on the Isle of Wight was this exciting. I'd have brought my tranquillisers.'

He looked so relaxed that Felice had to fight down a bubble of laughter before she could reply, 'Life here is one long tranquilliser…more peaceful than exciting. Do you have any children?'

'Not that I know of.' Tobias glanced at her profile with a puzzled frown creasing his forehead.

'Damn,' Felice breathed. 'I was depending on your having children. Next you'll be telling me you're not even married.'

'I'm not.' He swivelled his big bulk in his seat to study her more closely. 'Should I be?'

'Yes! The island has a lot to offer a married man with children. I'm not so sure about a bachelor. You might be bored stiff and then you won't want to stay.'

'Do you want me to stay?'

'Gosh, yes!' she exclaimed, sounding more sixteen than twenty-six.

'I'm flattered.'

'You might not be when you know the reason,' she confessed.

There was a pause while Tobias assimilated this, then he suggested, 'Why don't you sock it to me straight? A few minutes with you has made me as shock-proof as I'm ever going to be.'

They'd reached the top of the cliffs. Ahead of them were the wind-frothed waves of the grey, wintry sea. Not exactly a sight to encourage a stranger that the island was a good place to live. Felice turned the car so that they faced the valley, heaved on the handbrake, and repeated in dismay, 'Shock-proof? I'm not that bad, am I?'

'I wasn't thinking of bad, just different,' Tobias replied, and his voice sounded vibrant in the silence that enveloped them as she cut the engine.

Felice grimaced. 'You mean I'm not the sort of woman you meet every day of the week?'

He smiled. 'I should think once in a lifetime would be enough.'

'My turn to be shot down in flames,' Felice sighed, more resigned than surprised. She knew she had her faults.

'I meant that as a compliment.'

She didn't belive him for a minute but she appreciated his tact so much that she said impulsively, 'Tobias, you're too nice for your own good. It's only fair to warn you that I'm a bossy, managing sort of woman. When I want something, I don't take prisoners. If you don't watch out, I'll take merciless advantage of you. I won't be able to help myself. It's the way I am.'

'If it's my body you're after, you'd better let me arrange the time and place,' he drawled. 'The spirit's willing but the car's inadequate. We're both too big.'

Felice was so taken aback she was struck dumb, then she began to giggle helplessly, innocently unaware of how attractive he found the sound. 'That wasn't why I kidnapped you,' she managed at last, gesturing to the valley spread out below them. 'I just wanted to show you Woodlands.'

'Is that all?' Tobias sounded disappointed. 'I saw it from the air.'

'Phooey!' she scoffed. 'You can't get the atmosphere of the valley from up there.'

'Do I need to?'

'Of course you do! It would be a crime if you came here, looked at the Hall and went away again without getting the feel of the estate. You might put it straight on the market without realising what a gem it is, and that would be a tragedy!'

'A tragedy for whom?' he asked.

'Me,' Felice admitted, making the mistake of looking him squarely in the eyes and finding she couldn't lie. She added hastily, 'But it could be for you, too. Just look down there—really look.'

'I'm looking,' Tobias said, sounding bored. 'What am I supposed to be seeing?'

'You are seeing Woodlands in winter,' she scolded, as though she were a schoolmarm with a particularly dim pupil to instruct. 'That's at its worst, but it's still quite a place. It's zoned as an area of outstanding beauty, you know.'

Carried away by her own enthusiasm, she made a sweeping gesture with her hand that encompassed the entire valley. 'There's everything you could possibly wish for here. Woods, marshes, pastures, arable fields, streams, beaches and cliffs. Heck,' she added, 'it's even got its own neat little airstrip without ruining the view.

In spring, it's breathtaking. In summer, it's a little paradise. In autumn——'

'Where's the Hall?' Tobias interrupted.

Felice frowned at him, unwilling to talk about the house yet. Deciding she had no choice, she pointed reluctantly to her right. 'See that wood? It's on a rise so it hides the Hall from here. The Hall was built on the far side, to take advantage of a particularly fine view of the sea across the meadows. Now as I was saying, in autumn the valley is——'

'All right, I'm sold on the view,' he interrupted again. 'What's wrong with the Hall?'

Felice, realising again that for all his friendliness Tobias wasn't an easy man to side-track, decided to call a halt to the sightseeing. She needed to play for time while she figured out the most tactful way to answer his question.

She started up the engine and drove back down into the valley. When they rejoined the meandering lane that passed for the main road, she switched the meter on again and temporised, 'Why do you suppose there's something wrong with the Hall?'

'Because you showed me the view first. That suggests the view's a winner and the Hall's a loser...unless, of course, you kidnap all your customers for the sheer hell of taking them on the scenic route.'

'You weren't born yesterday, were you?' she asked, more under her breath than anything, but he heard.

'Just as well we've got that one sorted out.'

Felice glanced quickly at him. Was there a warning note in his voice? Or was she imagining things? She felt a twinge of unease but she was too far into this to draw back now, so she shrugged and went on as breezily as she could, 'Don't run away with the idea that there's anything wrong with the Hall. There isn't. It's just a bit—different.'

'Like you?' he suggested.

'Hardly!' she retorted. 'The Hall's mock gothic. Most of it, anyway.'

'Don't you mean it's a folly?'

'Somebody's got to you before I have,' Felice exclaimed indignantly. 'You might have said.'

'I've done my homework, if that's what you mean, but I'd rather have your opinion. It's got to be more refreshing than the piles of documents I've waded through. You don't mind if I find you—refreshing?'

'N-no,' Felice stuttered. There was no warning in his voice now, quite the reverse. He'd spoken with a warmth, almost an intimacy, that made her feel strangely light-headed. She put it down to missing breakfast, and forced herself to concentrate on essentials.

'About the Hall,' she began again. 'I admit it's been called a folly, but only because it's one of those places you either love or hate. It all depends on how much imagination you have.'

'Are you sure you don't mean taste?' Tobias asked. 'I've read a comprehensive description of the place.'

'Oh, all right then, taste,' Felice agreed, ready to concede a point in the hope that he wasn't noticing how slowly she was driving. She was still playing for time. She had so much to discuss with him but nothing was working out as she'd planned.

Tobias Hunter seemed so relaxed and obliging, but it was beginning to dawn on her that he, not she, was manipulating the situation she'd created. What was he then—a sleeping tiger? She shuddered deliciously as a thrill swept over her, raising goose-pimples on flesh that was far from cold.

Again she called herself to order, worried that she could blow this heaven-sent opportunity to come to a firm agreement with him if she fell into the sex trap. That wasn't what she wanted at all, and yet she almost felt as though he were luring her into it.

She couldn't be sure, because he was far too subtle. Never having come across his particular brand of charm and challenge before, she wasn't certain about anything.

Sometimes, though, she got the distinct feeling he was playing with her. Did tigers play before they pounced?

Again Felice shuddered, but then she remembered that other feeling she'd had about him, the feeling that she'd found a friend. It helped her to dismiss a sudden premonition that everything between her and Tobias wasn't as straightforward as it seemed. Or, rather, that he wasn't as straightforward as he appeared to be.

Convincing herself that her imagination was working overtime, she relaxed, relinquishing his challenge so that she could enjoy his charm.

'What about your taste?' he asked.

Taste? she thought, confused. Then she fell in. 'Oh, you mean the Hall! In that respect, I don't think I have any, because I adore the place. When I was a child I used to wish I lived there instead of on its doorstep, so to speak. That's why I was hoping you'd be married with children. They would have loved the Hall for its own sake, and to blazes with the purists.'

Slowly as she was driving, they had to arrive some time. As she braked reluctantly in front of the massive iron gates barring the driveway, she asked, 'Are you a purist?'

'Ask me after I've seen the Hall,' Tobias snapped, his mood changing so suddenly that she was taken aback. Before she could adjust, he went on, 'What are we waiting here for? I've admired the view; can I skip admiring the gates?'

Felice, normally the most easygoing of people, surprised herself by snapping back, 'Certainly, just as soon as you produce the key to open the padlock. I drive a taxi. I'm not a locksmith.'

Instead of reaching in his pockets or his briefcase, or wherever he had the keys, Tobias put a hand under her chin and turned her face towards his. 'You're mad at me,' he said, looking deeply into her eyes.

If there was one thing Felice couldn't stand, it was being pawed by her customers, but this was different. Tobias's voice was soft, his strong fingers gentle, and his expression was...was...tender? It was another mercurial change of mood she couldn't adjust to.

'You were mad at me first,' she grumbled, 'and I've no idea why.'

'Stop wishing I was married and I'll stop getting mad,' he told her.

Felice wanted to ask him why, but he released her chin to open his briefcase, and the moment was lost. He brought out two ornate keys, each big enough to have opened the Tower of London.

They said together, 'They're never going to fit that padlock.'

They looked at each other and smiled, and the tension that had flared so unexpectedly between them vanished as though it had never been. Felice felt warm and happy again. She switched off the meter and said, 'Over the wall it is, then. I know a place.'

'Somehow that doesn't surprise me.' Tobias switched on the meter again. 'If I want your company, which I do, I'll pay for it.'

Felice shook her head and switched the meter back off. 'The business part of the ride is over. As a friend, I'm not for hire.'

Tobias looked at her long and hard, then nodded. 'Fair enough,' he said, 'so long as you don't lose your job over it.'

'I'm self-employed,' she replied, getting out of the car and going round to open his door, but he was out before she got there. 'I'm not really supposed to be working this morning, because I was on the disco run last night.'

He stood looking down at her, an experience she quite enjoyed—for novelty's sake, she supposed—and then he asked, 'The disco run?'

'That's what I call it,' she replied, waiting for him to fall in beside her, then beginning to walk along the grass verge that edged the high stone wall guarding the privacy of Woodlands Hall. 'Saturday night revellers need transport home because of the drink-driving laws. It's a busy time for taxi drivers.'

'What time did you get to bed last night?'

'You mean this morning! Somewhere around two. I'm not normally on call again until ten, but the driver who was supposed to collect you had a breakdown. A lucky stroke for me.'

Tobias frowned. 'Do you need the work that badly?'

She laughed up at him. 'This particular job is more than work. As soon as I heard who'd made the booking I was out of bed in a flash. I've been breaking my neck to meet you.'

'Why?'

'You're my landlord.'

'Am I indeed?' he murmured, giving her an assessing look she couldn't make head or tail of. 'Is that why you're so friendly?'

'No, but it might have been. You made it easy by being nice.'

'I get the distinct impression you're buttering me up for something,' he replied cautiously.

'What a suspicious mind you've got!'

'Put it down to experience,' he retorted. 'I gather you live somewhere on the estate?'

'Yes, just down the road at Woodlands Cottage, and I want to go on living there. That's why it's so important to me that you move into the Hall. If you sell the estate I'll be chucked out. I'm already under notice to quit. The solicitors served that on me before they knew there was an heir. If the estate is broken up, the cottage will be worth more without a tenant.'

'I knew you had to have some kind of ulterior motive,' he said, and he didn't look happy about it.

'I could have played coy, but I reckon we understand each other well enough by now for plain speaking. It saves a lot of time.' A qualm struck her and she added, 'I am right in judging you as a man who prefers frankness, aren't I?'

'Yes.'

His answer was a bit brief but it was the right one. Felice sighed with relief. The worst was over, but the negotiating would have to wait because they'd reached a place where the grass on the verge gave way to a tree and an outcrop of bushes.

She pushed her way through the bushes and held them apart for Tobias to follow. 'This is it,' she said. 'We climb the tree and step off on to the wall. We have to jump down the other side, but that's no big deal.'

'Do you want a lift up?' he asked.

'Heavens, no!' she exclaimed, nimbly climbing from branch to branch with the ease of long experience. 'I've been doing this since I was a child. Just follow me and you won't even get your boots scuffed. Well, not much, anyway.'

Tobias looked up at her rounded bottom and long legs encased provocatively in tight jeans, then looked away and counted to ten. The minx, he thought. She had to know what she was doing to him! He counted another ten and began to follow.

It was only when Felice stepped on to the wall that she realised what an opportunity she'd missed. Drat! If she'd been a strictly feminine female she'd have played helpless and let him help her. It might have helped her cause. Men always went soppy when they had a helpless woman on their hands, and she could do with all the help she could get in persuading Tobias to do what she wanted.

Her second thoughts had come much too late, though. He was already on the wall beside her. They both sat down and looked at the drop. 'The safest way is to turn, hold on to the wall, ease your body down and then let go,' she instructed. 'It's not much of a drop then, not for people as tall as you and I are.'

Tobias looked at her in irritation. 'I said I appreciated frankness, not stating the obvious.'

'Sorry,' she apologised. 'That's the bossy part of me showing again. I was always that way inclined but I suppose bringing up the children made me worse.'

'What children?' he demanded.

'Janetta, Garth and Gavin. My sister and twin brothers. I've been their guardian since my parents died.'

'When was that?'

'Eight years ago—long enough for me to get set in my managing ways,' she replied in wry self-mockery. 'The twins were only eight at the time, and Janetta ten—much too young to fight back.'

'Are they fighting back now?'

'Not that I've noticed; not yet, anyway.'

'Well, I fight back,' Tobias growled.

Felice only laughed. 'That I have noticed. At the risk of sounding bossy again, I think we should get off this wall. We're melting the frost and it's getting wet. Better throw down your briefcase first, then——'

'Stop telling me what to do!' he snapped.

'Sorry.' She reached out and touched his cheek in an instinctive effort to pacify him. 'I really am.' She saw the irritation fade from his face, couldn't figure out the expression that replaced it, and didn't hang around to find out. Any moment the wetness of the wall would seep through her jeans. She turned and dropped lightly into a mulch of decaying leaves.

Tobias, still feeling the sensuous touch of her fingers on his cheek, again counted to ten, then threw down his briefcase and dropped beside her. Felice was stooping to pick up his briefcase but he got to it first and growled, 'Stop doing things for me, too.'

'Sorry,' she said again. 'Because I'm big, people usually expect me to——'

'I don't,' he butted in, 'and I'm bigger.'

Felice felt light-headed again, and fluttery with it. This must be the way dainty women felt when men wouldn't let them do the smallest thing. What had she been missing all these years? Whatever it was, she'd finally met a man big and powerful enough to redress the balance...

Horrified at the way her thoughts were turning, she began to march over the leaves and through the trees towards the driveway in a way that would have done credit to a guardsman, unable to come to terms with how feminine and fragile Tobias made her feel. It was so novel, she was afraid of making a fool of herself.

Tobias marched beside her and, because she was peculiarly sensitive to him, she guessed he was still annoyed. Yet why should he be? He'd said himself that his manhood was too secure to feel threatened by the likes of her.

Abandoning imponderables, she said candidly, 'If I make a real effort to stop bossing you about, do you think you could bury the hatchet somewhere other than my head?'

They'd reached the driveway and the going was easier, but Tobias stopped and looked down at her. 'Right now your head seems the proper place for it.'

Felice gave way to another impulse, saying with a teasing laugh, 'You never say what I expect you to. I find that very refreshing. You don't mind if I find you refreshing?' She grinned cheekily at him, and they both knew she was mocking him with his own words.

'Where's that hatchet?' he asked, but she could see the amusement in his grey eyes.

'Still in my head, apparently,' she returned, laughing outright. She slipped her arm through his in the friendly way that was so much a part of her and began to draw him on towards the house. 'Now we're friends again, can we talk about my cottage?'

'Don't you mean mine?'

'You're not going to be disagreeable, are you?' she murmured, glancing up at him from under her long eyelashes. Obsessed with sorting out her tenancy, she didn't give a thought to how seductive she looked, but Tobias did.

After a long pause, he replied, 'Just stating facts. You should try it some time.'

'All right,' Felice agreed equably, 'facts you can have, although it's a tricky situation. In a sense you're my landlord, and in a sense you're not, you see.'

'No, I don't see,' Tobias told her, wondering how her eyelashes could look so long and lustrous without a trace of mascara on them. 'You'd better spell it out for me.'

Felice took her last fence at a rush. 'I don't pay any rent.'

'You mean you're a squatter?'

'Yes,' she agreed. 'Dreadful, isn't it? I've got the rent banked, all eight years of it, but Old Josh would never take it. I wish he had, because it means I haven't any rights of tenancy at all. Unless you keep the estate and put the tenancy on a regular footing, I have to get out, and I can't afford to.'

'Shouldn't you be ankle-deep in snow and playing a violin?' he asked caustically. 'That's the right background for a fair maiden pleading with the wicked landlord, isn't it?'

Felice gurgled with laughter. 'Fancy me missing a trick or two like that!'

'I don't think you've missed many others,' he answered bluntly.

Her smile faded and she frowned at him. 'You're serious, aren't you?'

'Aren't you?'

'Well, yes, but though I'd love to stay on in the cottage, I only strictly need it for another two years. That's not too much to ask, is it?'

'What's so special about two years?' Tobias asked, watching her closely.

'That's when my brothers leave school and go to university. Janetta's due to go this autumn, so she's nearly off my hands. If only your great-uncle had hung in there for a couple more years, everything would have been fine.'

Felice's big blue eyes, full of appeal, held his as she bit her lip and continued, 'It was very awkward for me, Old Josh dropping dead like that.'

'I don't suppose he was too keen about it, either.'

Felice gasped, then giggled. When she could, she apologised, 'Sorry, I didn't mean that quite the way it sounded. I must have seemed very selfish.'

'We all have our own corner to fight for.'

'I suppose we do.' She thought for a moment, then went on innocently, 'You must be wondering why your great-uncle wouldn't take my rent.'

'Surprise me,' Tobias suggested cynically.

CHAPTER THREE

SURPRISE him? It was Felice who was surprised. Whatever could Tobias mean, and why did he sound so—so hostile all of a sudden? Had she missed something somewhere? She blinked at him, baffled.

Deciding her senses must be picking up vibes that really weren't there, she shook her head in bewilderment and said, 'I don't know about surprise, although I suppose it is an unusual story. My father was the official tenant of the cottage, but when he and my mother were lost at sea——'

She paused involuntarily. Eight years ago, yet still the tragedy had the power to hurt. She didn't like talking about it, even to a man she felt drawn to like Tobias. But she had to. It was the only way to make him understand the tangled situation she was in.

Felice pulled herself together and went on resolutely, 'My parents were a mad, impulsive pair. That's what made them so lovable. My younger sister Janetta's very much like them, in personality and talent. Anyway, they were seascape painters and——'

'Not very successful ones, I gather, if they couldn't even afford their own home,' Tobias broke in.

For a moment Felice was piqued. Then she supposed he was entitled to make that sort of comment since money was something they'd have to discuss soon. 'They did all right,' she replied quietly. 'They just weren't hung up on possessions. They preferred to spend their money

34

on education rather than a house, and educating four children privately doesn't come cheap.'

'But renting Woodlands Cottage did?'

'Yes, but it's an ancient cottage, much older than the Hall. In fact, it was the original farmhouse for this land before the Hall was built. Anything that old needs caring tenants. Besides, Old Josh was always eccentric, even before he got so odd towards the end. He hated strangers around him and the cottage had been empty for years. It was falling apart when my parents discovered it. For some reason, he took to them and let them rent it.'

Probably because of Mother, Felice thought privately. She'd had the ability to charm the birds out of the trees—an ability she herself could do with right now. Tobias wasn't making this as easy as she'd hoped.

'And then?' he prompted.

'Then,' Felice replied, unaware of the dreamy, reminiscent smile touching her lips, 'the dust flew. Literally. As I said, the cottage was in a bad way and needed taking apart and putting together again. My earliest memories are of us living more or less like gypsies while one room after another was renovated.'

'At my great-uncle's expense?' Tobias asked pointedly.

'Heavens, no! My parents paid, and were happy to do so because it was such a lovely place to bring up a family. I wasn't much more than a tot at the time but my parents always intended to have more children. Janetta and the twins were longer coming than they'd expected, that's all.'

Felice looked up at Tobias anxiously, afraid he was getting bored. The driveway to the Hall was pretentiously long, and they were walking slowly, but she'd wanted to get the business of the cottage sorted out before they got to the final bend.

She'd never intended to tell him her entire family history, but one thing had led to another, as it always seemed to with Tobias.

She didn't think he looked impatient. In fact, she couldn't read his expression at all. She took that as a good sign and rushed on, 'Anyway, when I was away at college studying horticulture, my parents took out their sailing dingy. It was a gusty October afternoon and bad weather was forecast. They trusted to luck, as they so often did, but their luck ran out. The storm struck sooner than expected. Nobody really knows what happened, but their bodies were washed up two days later.'

A sigh she couldn't repress escaped her. 'The only comfort is that they were together when it happened. That's the way they would have wanted it.'

She was glad Tobias didn't say anything trite, but stuck to practicalities. 'So you dropped out of college and you took over the family?' he asked.

Felice nodded, grateful for his understanding. 'Yes— and that's when I tried to take over the tenancy of the cottage. The problem was, Old Josh refused to see me. Of course, he was virtually a recluse by then.'

'I'd heard he was a bit odd,' Tobias agreed.

'He was frozen in time, and everybody else had to be, too,' Felice elaborated bluntly. 'He wouldn't have anything to do with change at all. When somebody quit his staff, he wouldn't hire a replacement. That's why the estate got so run down. The funny thing was——'

She broke off, wondering if she was being a bit too blunt. After all, she was speaking of one of Tobias's relatives.

'Don't stop there. Tell me what was funny,' Tobias said, and she thought she must have imagined the sceptical note in his voice, because she couldn't see any reason for it.

'Well, although he wouldn't see me so I could legally take over the tenancy, he didn't do anything to evict me and the children,' she continued. 'He just acted as though we weren't there. I think that must have been his way of preserving the status quo. Naturally, we stayed on in the cottage.'

'Naturally,' Tobias mimicked.

Felice, not looking for double meanings, accepted his comment at face value and concluded thankfully, 'So now you know why your great-uncle's death left us in such a pickle. The cottage is still home to the younger children during school vacations.'

Tobias's dark eyebrows drew together. 'You mean all three are at boarding-school? That must cost a packet.'

'It does,' Felice admitted freely, 'but I'm just carrying out my parents' wishes. They wanted the younger children to have the same educational advantages that I had.'

'Did they leave enough money for that?'

'They left some, but not enough.'

'Then paying no rent must have been a godsend to you,' he drawled laconically.

'The rent is banked,' Felice repeated, a tiny frown creasing her own brow as she went on the defensive. 'It's not my fault if Old Josh wouldn't take it. It's yours any time you want it.'

'Have you increased the amount to allow for inflation?'

'Well, no, but you're welcome to the interest it's made. It was never my intention to take advantage of your great-uncle's oddness.'

'Very high-minded of you,' Tobias observed cynically.

To his surprise, Felice chuckled. 'More desperate-minded, actually. Nobody can predict what eccentrics will do, and it was always possible Old Josh would suddenly demand the rent. I didn't want to be caught on the hop. It was the same sense of self-preservation that made me want to talk to you before you came to a decision about the estate.'

There was a lengthy silence, then Tobias demanded, 'What exactly do you want from me?'

Felice turned wondering eyes up at him again. Surely she'd imagined that suddenly harsh note in his voice? What the devil could he think she wanted apart from a lease for the cottage? 'I've already told you. A legal tenancy for two years.'

'What's wrong with indefinitely?' he asked, watching her closely.

Felice's hopes soared and she responded eagerly, 'Indefinitely would be lovely, of course!'

'I thought it might be.'

Again, she thought she must have imagined the underlying sarcasm in his reply, and again she dismissed it because she was so overjoyed that he had raised the prospect of her staying on in the cottage for as long as she wanted. Oh, how marvellous that would be! It had been her home ever since she could remember, and she didn't want to move.

She simply couldn't imagine any place nicer to live than on the unspoiled Woodlands Estate. Such places were vanishing so fast she almost felt like a dinosaur, doomed to extinction when its natural environment vanished. Involuntarily, she shivered.

With her arm through his, Tobias felt the tremor. 'What's the matter?' he asked.

Felice very nearly told him, then erred on the side of caution. He might think her some kind of nut, and she didn't want him getting the idea everybody in the valley was as weird as Old Josh had been. That wouldn't exactly encourage him to make his home here!

'I asked what was the matter?' he repeated, looking down at her intently.

'I—er—was just thinking how funny it is the way things work out. If only Old Josh had lived for a couple more years, I wouldn't have had to burden you with my problems. It's not very fair on you, is it?'

No need to say any more, she thought. If Tobias didn't know where she was coming from by now, he never would. Besides, she didn't visualise any problem there. Hadn't she sensed from the start that they were on the same wavelength?

At that moment, her foot caught in a bramble that had strayed over the drive and rooted itself among the weeds. It held firm and she tripped. Her arm was still through Tobias's and she clutched at him as she began to fall. Instinctively, he reached out to save her.

Suddenly she was in his arms.

It was entirely by accident but it gave her a taste of his strength. First she'd lost her footing, and now she lost her head. She simply couldn't help herself. There was something in his powerful hold that taught her what it was like to feel utterly defenceless and yet completely secure at one and the same time.

It was a feeling she'd never experienced before, and it was heady stuff. Her breath caught in her throat, her cheeks flushed and her wondering eyes stared un-guardedly into his. Suddenly she knew that she wanted him to kiss her, wanted—needed!—to feel his firm lips against her soft ones. Blissfully, she also knew it was what he wanted, too.

She read his need in the darkening of his eyes, felt it in the tightening of his arms around her. Responsively, she clung to him, feeling her soft body crush deliciously against the hard length of his. Her eyes closed in willing and unthinking surrender.

Tobias looked at the long sweep of dark eyelashes shadowing her flushed cheeks, the wayward tendrils of hair escaping from her plait to gleam like gold against her perfect complexion, and bent his head to claim her waiting lips.

Then he hesitated. His lips had actually brushed hers, awakening wild and wayward promises of satisfaction to come, when he changed his mind and thrust her away from him.

Felice, totally unprepared, couldn't adjust quickly enough. Dazed and disbelieving, she stumbled and almost fell. She could still feel the strength of his arms around her, the imprint of his powerful thighs against hers, the tantalisingly feather-light touch of his lips. Most of all, she could still feel his desire—a desire he had killed with cold and callous deliberation.

Why?

One moment she'd been hovering on the brink of paradise, the next she was out in the cold. It was too much to come to terms with. She simply didn't know what had happened, what had gone wrong. There were no words she could say, none she could even think of. She could only raise large, bewildered eyes to Tobias, mutely questioning.

It was then she saw that the heat had gone from his. Not even the warmth of friendship remained. She was looking at a cold-eyed stranger—a stranger Tobias had

never been, not even at the very beginning when they
had shaken hands and introduced themselves. It was as
though they'd already known each other then, had
always known each other.

Now, when she'd thought deepening attraction had
forged them into so much more than friends, they were
strangers. It was crazy. But it was happening. Had
happened.

She felt exposed, shamed, naked.

Slowly and painfully, she began to recover. She'd been
rejected. Whatever else she couldn't understand, she
could understand that. She had been thrust away like so
much unwanted baggage. Her pride flickered like a
flame, ousting desire, wrapping its protective cover about
her, finding reasons for her behaviour—behaviour that
had previously seemed so natural, and now seemed
inexplicably fast.

She summoned up a parody of a smile and said, 'Sorry,
I tripped. There was a root...'

That didn't explain why she'd clung to him, of course,
or why she'd melted against him and waited to be kissed,
but he'd encouraged her! She'd never have behaved like
that otherwise. Still, whatever had made him change his
mind and thrust her away, she expected him to help her
over her embarrassment. Out of humanity, if nothing
else. She was wrong.

'I don't see any root,' Tobias said.

They both looked down. There were plenty of weeds,
but the root that had ensnared her boot was hidden
among them. Felice wasn't going to get down on her
hands and knees to search for it. She'd already de-
meaned herself enough, and reaction was setting in with
a vengeance.

'It's there,' she replied shortly. 'I don't make a habit of throwing myself into men's arms.'

'I'm glad to hear it, especially when I'm around. I prefer to take the initiative. In fact, I insist on it. The sooner you learn that, the better we'll get on.'

'I don't know what you mean,' she exclaimed, even more bewildered than before.

'Then I'll spell it out for you so you don't make the same mistake again. It never pays to overplay your hand with me. You started off all right, but you've been coming on to me stronger and stronger, and I don't like being pressured—sexually or otherwise. Try for a bit of subtlety to keep the illusion alive a little longer.'

'Wh-what illusion?' she stuttered, not really believing she was hearing all this.

'That you're a nice, sweet country kid who doesn't want anything from me. All right, so we both know that you do, but the illusion was nice while it lasted. It's a pity you had to blow it with too much body language. It made you into just another "gimme" girl and, frankly, I've got those queuing up for me. If you want to keep your entertainment value, try to keep the novelty appeal you had back there at the beginning.'

Felice's soft lips parted in indignation. 'Why, you— you arrogant——' She couldn't go on. What he'd said was so preposterous that words failed her. When she recovered the power of speech, she stuttered, 'How dare you suggest I was—was—throwing myself at you? I'd never——!' It was no use. As her indignation deepened into outrage, words failed her again.

Tobias's dark eyebrows lifted sceptically. 'You mean I imagined that coy little kidnap, that provocative waggling of your butt in my face as you climbed the tree, that clinging on to my arm, that hurling yourself in my arms? Oh, come on, Felice! We both know I'm quite a catch, and that isn't vanity, it's stating a fact.'

'If you imagine I'm trying to catch you——!'

'One way or the other,' he broke in wearily. 'Your problem is that your tactics are strictly amateurish compared with some of the tricks women have played on me through the years. My problem is that I'm too experienced not to recognise the syndrome, and I'm bored out of my mind by it.'

'There wasn't any syndrome,' she denied hotly. 'I—I wasn't trying to flirt with you.'

'You mean it never crossed your mind that as a woman you might get more out of me if you used your body than if you stayed strictly impersonal?' he demanded.

Felice opened her mouth to deny any such thing, then closed it again. She couldn't deny it! Not when she remembered how she'd wished she'd played helpless when she'd climbed that tree—because it might have helped her to win Tobias round to her way of seeing things about the lease.

It had been innocent enough, but, interpreted his way, it took on a whole new meaning—but only to a man with an overbearing ego! But it wasn't fair. She was nothing like the women he described. Nothing!

All the same, as the silence lengthened between them, hot shame spread its tell-tale story across her cheeks. She could only mumble helplessly, 'It wasn't like that.'

'It never is,' he replied cynically.

Felice fumed. First he'd rejected her, then he'd humiliated her, and now he was mocking her. Her so-called friend. How dared he! She wanted desperately to hold on to her anger but the hurt she felt almost destroyed her by whimpering, How *could* he?

Tears stung her eyes. She felt so betrayed, and there was never any defence against betrayal. The only help she had was a fierce determination to never, ever, expose herself to being so humiliated again. Whatever happened, there wouldn't be any more unguarded moments with Tobias Hunter!

It was that determination that steeled her to turn away from him. It was a rejection of her own, and she hoped he knew it. Her head held high, she walked on.

Later on she would figure out why war and not love had been declared between them. For the moment, it was enough for her to know that it was war...

They turned the final bend in the driveway and there, spread out in all its conflicting glory, was Woodlands Hall. 'Good God!' Tobias exclaimed, stopping dead in his tracks. 'Is this for real?'

It was a bit much to take in all at once, Felice supposed. If they'd still been friends, she would have smiled at his shock and set about cajoling him into seeing the Hall as she did—as a place of enchantment.

But hostility still crackled between them and she concentrated instead on how strange it was to be standing here in the open, with no fear of being shouted at and chased away.

Always before, when she'd been growing up and the mystery of the forbidden Hall had drawn her like a magnet, she'd had to skulk in the bushes to see it—a trespasser.

Strangely, she felt as though this big man standing beside her was the trespasser now, and she was the one who belonged. Probably because she loved the place. Time hadn't altered that in any way. The Hall still intrigued and enchanted her, just as Tobias had such a few short heartbeats ago...

She felt a strange, sad tug of loss. The feeling she'd met a kindred soul had been so marvellous while it had lasted! A sigh welled up within her but she forced it down. If Tobias's opinion of himself was so great he actually believed she'd deliberately thrown herself at him, then he really wasn't worth bothering about.

He and his ego could have a beautiful relationship, and heaven help any poor woman who tried to come between them. It certainly wouldn't be her. From here on in, her sole interest in Tobias Hunter was wangling a lease out of him for the cottage.

She wished, she really wished, she could say stuff the cottage, and leave him here in this neglected wilderness, but she had to be practical. Not for the first time, what she wanted to do had to come second to the needs of her family.

She simply had to hang on to the cottage! That was much more important than her bruised feelings. Finding another unfurnished house large enough, and at a rent she could afford, was virtually impossible. She'd already tried when she'd first been given notice to quit. People simply didn't want tenants with teenagers, dogs and cats, and she was encumbered with them all.

No, not encumbered, she corrected herself hastily. She'd opted to take over the family. Even if a relative had offered to take on the younger children, she wouldn't have let them. They were a *family*. Anyway, she'd never had any regrets, and Tobias wasn't going to make her start feeling sorry for herself at this late stage.

It might have been eight years of hard graft, but it had been fun, too, and she'd never been bored. She'd thrived on the challenges, and Tobias Hunter was just another challenge. If she had to crawl around him to preserve the family home for a little while longer, then, all right, she'd do it.

Felice was trying to figure out how she could crawl and still preserve some tatters of her already badly mauled dignity when Tobias found his voice again. 'What the hell is it supposed to be?' he asked scathingly, 'I've never seen such a bastardisation of incompatible styles.'

That wasn't what Felice wanted to hear, mostly because it was true. Somehow she had to soften his contempt so that he could come to appreciate the glory as well as the folly of his inheritance. 'Bastardisation,' she repeated, purely to give herself time to think. 'I think you've just made that word up.'

He shot her a baleful look. 'Whoever built this place made it up.'

'You'll feel differently about it when you know its history.'

'I don't need to know its history,' he scowled.

'Of course you do! You own it.' Felice began to walk forward again, glad to have something to talk about that was as far removed from the abortive kiss as it was possible to be. She heard rather than saw Tobias striding to catch up with her.

He said between set teeth, 'Haven't you learned yet that it doesn't pay to be bossy with me?'

'If you expect me to change the habits of a lifetime just to please you, then you expect too much.'

'I don't expect anything from you,' he replied crushingly. 'You're the one who expects something from me.'

He had her there. Felice seethed, then she said hotly, 'All I expect from you at the moment is to listen to a little of the Hall's history. It might help you to understand something for once, instead of the snarling and scoffing you're so good at.'

Not giving him chance to think of another crushing reply, she rushed on, 'Woodlands Hall was built at the end of the eighteenth century by a merchant who'd made his fortune in India. That explains the cupola over the central building, the shape of the windows and the minarets at each corner.'

Tobias butted in sarcastically, 'What explains the two wings? They look like a pair of cut-down castles stuck on to a miniature Taj Mahal.'

'I'm getting to those,' Felice replied, switching to a soothing tone that rattled him more than being snapped at. She studied the squat, crenellated towers that guarded the equally squat wings, and continued, 'They're supposed to look like castles. There was a gothic revival going on when the Hall was built. Our merchant, though, obviously wanted a bit of India as well as a bit of old England, so he built both.'

'Our merchant,' Tobias repeated mockingly, 'had more money than sense.'

Felice scowled at him. 'I like to think he had a dream, and he built that dream regardless of what anybody thought or said. I find that very touching.'

'I find it nauseating. An Indian temple slapped between two sawn-off castles! Good Lord, you'd have to be eccentric to live here. I was prepared for a folly, but this is a monstrosity.'

'It's not a monstrosity!' Felice exclaimed passionately. 'I'm not the least bit eccentric and I'd love to live here.'

Tobias swung round and faced her. All the power of his big body seemed to blaze through his grey eyes as he stared searchingly at her. 'So that's it, is it?' he breathed. 'Your real ulterior motive at last.'

Felice didn't know what he was talking about but she hated the way his eyes were dissecting her. To think she'd once believed them warm, friendly, intimate. Now they were...insulting!

'Anybody with a grain of imagination would love to live in the Hall,' she defended, unsure where his attack was coming from but fighting back, anyway. 'Try it. You might find it grows on you.'

'Like a carbuncle?' he suggested.

His comment was so unexpected that she laughed. She really didn't want to, but she couldn't help herself. She thought his eyes softened momentarily, but she wasn't going to be deceived that way again. She quelled any answering softness and protested, 'That's not fair. The Hall might not be balanced and beautiful like a true architectural gem but——'

She was interrupted by his sudden shout of mocking laughter. She lifted her chin at him and continued doggedly, '—But it's a different kind of gem. It's a place where imagination runs riot, where things that shouldn't be possible have been made possible. It's—it's pure magic. You just have to give the magic time to work...'

Tobias was looking at her in a very different way now. She found her breath catching in her throat, then realised he was only mocking her when he said, 'Maybe I should hire you as my agent when I sell the place. I'm sure you'd do a good job on any passing sucker.'

Felice clenched her hands, her palms itching to slap his face, but he was turning away from her, getting out the two ornate keys. She was even irritated when he chose the right key to fit the lock of the massive front door.

Everything always seemed to go so right for him, and so wrong for her. Still, there was such a thing as a law of averages. He had to come unstuck some time. She found herself burning with a new sort of desire—to be around to see it!

CHAPTER FOUR

ALL the antagonism Tobias aroused within her was
driven from Felice's head as the door swung open and
they walked inside.

She stared around in disbelief. The Indian part of the
building was entirely an entrance hall, tiled from floor
to dome in blue and gold. There were a few pieces of
Indian furniture scattered about, but mostly there was
just an incredible feeling of space, tranquillity and
beauty.

Delicately arched windows let in shafts of grey, and
Felice could only imagine how magnificent it was when
the sun was shining. 'Heavens,' she whispered, awed,
her eyes widening into stars of wonder, 'if this is eccentric, then I'm all for eccentricity.'

Tobias didn't answer immediately, then he admitted,
'The inside beats the outside, but it hardly suits the
climate, does it? It's like a fridge in here.'

'Imagine it on a sunny day,' she replied, although
practical considerations were the last thing on her mind.

She didn't see his critical appraisal switch from the
splendour surrounding them to her rapt face. His eyebrows drew together. 'Haven't you been in here before?'

'Never.' She was so bewitched by all she was seeing
that she momentarily forgot he was her least favourite
person and slipped back into her old confiding ways.

'I had to trespass just to see the outside,' she explained. 'You know how impressionable children are.
I'd only ever seen Old Josh from a distance but I'd heard

about him, and he was like something out of a fairy story to me—an ogre. I felt I was taking my life into my hands just creeping around the grounds. I never had the courage to go as far as the windows in case I was caught and gobbled up.'

'I think even my great-uncle would have found you a bit of a mouthful,' Tobias murmured, as though he'd also forgotten the animosity between them.

Felice smiled. 'Oh, I wasn't quite so big then.'

'I wouldn't call you big. I'd say you were just r——' He broke off suddenly and frowned, as though he'd already said too much.

She found herself listening hopefully for him to continue. When he didn't, she swallowed the disappointment she shouldn't be feeling and concluded, 'When I grew up, of course, it would have been too embarrassing to be caught trespassing, so I never risked a peek inside the Hall then, either.'

'You're not trying to kid me you'd let embarrassment stop you doing anything you wanted to do, are you?' he asked sceptically.

Gosh, he really did think she was brazen, and probably depraved with it! What sort of women was he used to, for heaven's sake?

But her intrinsic honesty made her admit, 'There was another factor after my parents died. I thought if Old Josh caught sight of me he might remember about the cottage and chuck me out in a fit of rage. I'm probably doing him an injustice, and he wasn't really that awful, but I wasn't in any position to take risks.'

'You still aren't,' Tobias reminded her.

'You enjoy turning the screw, don't you? What is it with you—another notch, another laugh?'

'I don't get my kicks that way,' he denied. 'I just find it impossible to believe you fell in love with this place without setting foot inside. It doesn't make sense.'

Stung, she retorted, 'Don't you ever do or feel anything that other people don't understand?'

'No. I make sure everybody knows exactly where I'm at. It saves a lot of time, trouble and misunderstanding.'

'How boring,' she replied snootily.

It was Tobias's turn to be stung, and he snapped, 'Tell me exactly when I've bored you?'

'You just have.'

The temporary truce was definitely over. Tobias stared down at her, hostility flaring in his grey eyes. 'If you were a man, I'd say you had a lot of balls, and you were about to get them chopped off.'

Now they were really getting down to the nitty-gritty, she thought, determined not to be outraged, since that was clearly what he wanted. She took a deep breath and met his eyes squarely. 'But since I'm a woman . . . ?'

'I'll make allowances and say you have a lot of nerve.'

'Don't spare my feelings now,' she scoffed. 'I might never recover from the shock.'

His expression changed. She wasn't sure whether it was for the better and had further doubts when he continued, 'You've definitely got a certain entertainment value, Felice, but it would be a mistake to trade on it too much. Now let's look over the rest of this morgue.'

He began walking across the entrance hall to a door on the right, his footsteps echoing confidently in the silence. Spooks obviously didn't bother him, Felice thought as she caught up with him, but it wasn't very heartening to know that she didn't bother him much, either.

Drat the man, and he'd come so close to being her darling man, too! Oh, well, she'd have to write it all off to experience—if she survived. Now why did I think that? she wondered, and shivered.

'The cold getting to you?' he asked, glancing down at her.

'Yes.'

It was a fib and Tobias seemed to know it. He paused before leading her into one of the castle wings and said, 'I think you're scared there might be an ogre behind this door.'

'He couldn't be worse than the one I came in with.'

She was startled when Tobias smiled. She wished— oh, how she wished!—he didn't look so darned attractive when he smiled. 'One up to you,' he admitted, opening the door. 'I look forward to levelling up the score.'

Another shiver ran through Felice, although not for the world would she have admitted how much it stimulated and excited her. Again he saw it, but this time his smile wasn't so attractive. 'Precisely,' he almost purred. 'Now you don't know where or when I'm going to pounce, do you?'

Make what you like of that, Felice thought disgruntledly, as he strode away from her. Against her will, she found herself following him. If nothing else, he had a magnetism that she hadn't yet learned to resist.

They were in another hall. It was much smaller but the medieval theme came as a bit of a shock after the Indian splendour they'd just left.

Sightless suits of armour guarded the bottom of a solid oak staircase leading to a minstrels' gallery and the upper storey. 'As Alice said, it gets "curiouser and curiouser",' Tobias quoted, looking at the choice of doors leading from the intricately carved and heavily panelled walls.

'It gets more and more exciting,' Felice contradicted, her eyes sparkling. She thought of how many years she'd been itching to see inside this extravagant building, and how awful it would have been if she'd been disappointed. As it was, the revelation of each opening door was better than a birthday treat.

After that, apart from a few hurried comments, she didn't get much time to say anything as Tobias marched her through sitting-rooms, bedrooms, kitchens, utility-rooms, up and down towers, then back through the Indian hall to the other wing, which seemed strictly for guests.

Most of the furniture was shrouded in dust sheets—very spooky, but understandable enough. Old Josh had never been known to allow anybody over his doorstep, let alone entertain. Felice, longing to peek under the sheets, could have screamed with frustration as Tobias kept striding on as though he was trying to beat a stopwatch.

What drove the man? she wondered. Why come here at all if he wasn't really interested?

Worse, she knew the magic of this magnificent oddity that was Woodlands Hall hadn't touched him at all. Her own mind was full of kaleidoscopic impressions of grandeur, but she knew instinctively that his was as un-impressed as if he had no eyes to see, no senses to be touched by inspired folly and unashamed extravagance.

Strange, considering what enemies they'd turned out to be, that she should be so tuned in to reactions he hadn't even bothered to express.

Strange and frightening.

There was a long, low oak chest in the upstairs passage, warped and darkened with age. Felice sat down on it, determined to halt the hurricane that was Tobias Hunter. He might be egotistically overbearing, but he could scarcely keep on going and leave her here.

Or could he?

Felice found that not quite knowing what he would do added a delicious spice to her determination to make him appreciate fully what he would be losing if he swapped a unique place like Woodlands Hall for monetary gain.

Tobias, missing the sound of her footsteps behind him, swung round. 'Feet given out?' he asked.

'No.'

'Come on, then,' he said impatiently.

'No,' she repeated.

Tobias came back to her. 'What do you mean, no?'

'I want you to slow down, really consider what you've inherited here. You're refusing to see the Hall as anything but a folly, and that's blinding you to all the good things about it. Just stop looking it over with a closed mind. A closed mind is a dead mind!'

'I'll take a closed mind over a demented one any day.'

Looming over her as he was, she felt the power of him, but there was a certain wayward thrill in defying him. 'You just don't know how lucky you are,' she told him. 'Some people would do anything for a place like this.'

'We'll go into that later,' he baffled her by replying. 'In the meantime, let's move on before we're fossilised like the rest of this place.'

Felice found herself following him, her head in a whirl. Go into *what* later? No answer presented itself as she was whisked in and out of rooms again, and up and down more towers. Except, perhaps, that he was as odd as his great-uncle, but somehow she didn't think so.

The problem was she didn't know what to think. About anything at all. Her irritation was growing, though. To keep up with him, she had to hurry past so many things she would have loved to stop and examine in detail.

Had it been her inheritance, she could have spent a week in each wing alone, and still felt she'd missed a lot. Her curiosity was being teased, not satisfied. The thought came unbidden—and unappreciated—that Tobias was having the same effect on her, too.

She looked at his tall, burly form ahead of her and realised that here she was, going through a deserted mansion with a man she actually knew precious little about. All she was certain of was that lately she'd been over-exposed to his challenge and starved of his charm.

She found herself pining for his charm. She was missing that certain softness in his voice that weakened and bewitched her... the humour that made her feel he was a kindred soul... the smile that made his rugged face so heart-tuggingly handsome...

Well, all that had gone out of the window fast enough, she thought, pulling a face at her own gullibility. He was a Jekyll and Hyde. The charming man had vanished somewhere and she was left with a growling monster. She was wrong to hope for another transformation. She'd never be sure how long it would last. And yet... and yet... she did hope.

'What are you thinking?' Tobias asked suddenly.

'You wouldn't want to know.'

'That bad, is it?'

She bit her lip as his mouth curved into the smile she had been yearning to see—and didn't trust any more.

Her nerves still reacted to it, though, sending exciting messages over her susceptible body.

Felice, unsure whether she was about to be hit with charm or challenge, and not quite ready for either, looked away from him, and saw to her dismay that they were in a bedroom. The four carved posts of an ornate Jacobean bed rose solidly above a dust sheet lying over the mattress and covers.

With a sudden movement Tobias pulled the dust sheet away, exposing a faded patchwork quilt. 'Now you can sit down,' he said. 'I'm ready to listen to you.'

It was what Felice wanted, but this wasn't the setting she'd have chosen. She looked doubtfully from the bed to Tobias and hesitated.

'Don't tell me you're afraid?' he asked softly.

She was, but it was a fear of disillusion more than anything else. She hadn't known until this moment that she had any illusions left about Tobias, and it was disconcerting to find that she had. What was even more disconcerting was that she wanted to keep them.

For some crazy reason, the way he'd behaved up until now didn't matter as much as he was about to behave. She wanted to give him a second chance—and she wanted him to give her a second chance, too. The realisation stunned her.

Maybe it's the Hall, she thought frantically. Maybe there really is a kind of magic here that's temporarily bewitched me. Maybe when I get outside I'll be all right again.

Suddenly saw herself as he did, with her tongue moistening her dry lips, and realised he might well mistake it for a sexual signal. Confusion made her stutter, 'W-why should I be frightened?'

'You tell me,' he invited, sitting down on the bed and patting the place beside him. 'Come here and tell me.'

Felice hesitated, unsure of herself, unsure of him, unsure of everything.

'Now,' he added. It was a command, but he softened it by holding out his hand to her.

Felice couldn't find the strength or the will to resist his outstretched hand, and slowly she walked towards him and put her hand in his. It was an act of faith, but she had no idea whether she would be betrayed or not.

She felt his strong clasp, and then he was easing her down to sit beside him. His gentleness surprised her. It disarmed her, too, because she knew he was giving her the opportunity to pull away if she wanted to.

She knew she should have, but she felt strangely helpless. She'd known him such a little while, and yet she felt bound to him by ties she couldn't see and couldn't begin to understand.

'I'm going to kiss you,' he said. 'You know that, don't you?'

She nodded. Every fibre of her being had been aware of his intention from the moment he'd ordered her to come to him.

'Yet still you came to me,' he said softly.

'Yes.' Her voice was a sigh, a surrender, an acceptance of facts. Friends... enemies... whatever they were, she was incapable of resisting the magnetism that drew her to him. It was so strong, it was almost tangible.

He took her face between his big hands and studied her carefully. She thought she felt his strong fingers tremble slightly, but decided she must have imagined it as he bent his head to cover her lips with his. Surely she was the only one who was trembling! Not with fear—

never with fear!—but with anticipation so exquisite that it took her breath away.

His kiss was gentle, feather-light, deliciously exploratory, and it awoke such a blaze of response within Felice that her hands went involuntarily to his face.

She held him just as he was holding her, and as he raised his head to look at her again, she pulled his mouth down to hers and kissed him back with all the soul that ̣as in her. Her eyes closed. She almost wanted to weep, w̱ ̱re and so deep was the emotion flowing between so pṵ them.

It was incredible but somehow, somewhere, Tobias had become the most important person in her life. She'd have scoffed if anybody had told her such a thing could happen so quickly, but as their lips separated she smiled mistily at her own naïveté. Feeling like this didn't take *time*, it only took the right two people.

Tobias's lips had taught her that.

'What are you smiling about?' he asked, a frown cleaving a line between his eyebrows.

'Nothing,' she breathed, too shy to confess her feelings until he did first.

His frown deepened and she knew she'd said or done something wrong, but she didn't know what. Her bewilderment deepened when he said harshly, 'Well, don't smile too soon, Felice. Before I commit myself, I want a taste of what I'm getting into.'

As Felice's soft lips parted in surprise, he crushed them savagely beneath his own, his hands moving over her body as though he owned it. His change of mood was so sudden that she was too surprised to even struggle.

The exquisite feeling that had almost reduced her to tears by its sweetness just moments ago was swamped by a tide of passion he was forcefully arousing in her.

Even while she melted physically, mentally she froze, almost choking on the shock and disillusion of his abrupt change of mood.

This callous assault on her senses had nothing to do with caring. It was just an exercise in mastery, and it revolted her. 'Tobias please,' she begged, struggling to free herself. 'Please don't be such a brute! Let me go!'

'You don't mean that,' he mocked, tightening his grip on her and unbuttoning her coat. His hand slid under her jumper and his touch on her bare warm flesh made her gasp. Her nipples tautened, betraying her unwilling arousal, and relaying such excitement to the pit of her stomach that she couldn't stop herself from squirming ecstatically in his arms.

'Now call me a brute,' he murmured triumphantly, and crushed her lips again in a way that made any answer, defiant or submissive, impossible.

Brute, she whimpered silently. Brute...brute...brute...

She loathed what he was doing to her, loathed even more her pagan response, and yet when he pushed her back on the bed and bent his dark head to tantalise her nipples with his tongue, it took all her will power to force herself to go cold in his arms.

But she had to! She wanted so much more than his body. She wanted his love and respect. Anything less wasn't enough for her proud spirit. She wanted it all or nothing...and she knew now that nothing was what it was going to be.

Tobias had no real feeling for her—only the physical desire that made her feel cheap and tarnished. Revulsion at how nearly she'd become those two loathsome things made her drop her arms limply by her sides as she waited for his reaction.

Tobias raised his head from her breast and looked at her. It was a long, hard look but she met it unflinchingly. She guessed he must be wondering what part of her had been strong enough to resist him. She hoped, now his passionate grey eyes were cooling to stony flint, that he'd realise it was her integrity.

It became painfully obvious he realised no such thing when he said harshly, 'I detest women who turn it on and off like a tap, Felice.'

She was too upset to answer. She pulled down her sweater, closed her coat and rolled away from him. It was impossible to fight a man like Tobias on all the levels she'd fought him without feeling as though she'd been put through a wringer.

She stumbled to her feet while she still had the strength to do so. Her mind was numb, her legs weak. She felt as if Tobias had drawn the very life force out of her.

She staggered away from him, not towards the door and freedom, but to a high-backed Jacobean settle that wasn't shrouded with a sheet. She sat on the hard wooden seat, oblivious of the dust, trying to control her ragged breathing as she tidied her clothes and buttoned up her jacket.

Tobias, too, stood up. She watched with sad eyes while he walked towards the window and stood with his back towards her. The atmosphere between them was so tense that it almost choked her.

She knew she was being a fool, resting here like a wounded animal when she should be making a run for it, but she felt as much his captive as she had ever been. There was something in the very essence of the man that made her want to stay close to him, however much he disillusioned her.

Despairingly, she found herself accepting a very unpalatable truth—that Tobias would have to behave a great deal worse than he already had to drive her away from him.

And yet what worse could there be?

CHAPTER FIVE

TOBIAS turned from the window, his eyes seeking hers with the intensity that was so peculiarly his own. 'You were right,' he said abruptly. 'I was a brute. I'm sorry, I never meant to be.'

'I know,' she whispered, and was surprised to discover that she did.

'Thank you for that, anyway. I don't like myself too much at the moment.'

Felice's lips curved in a parody of her normally brilliant smile as she admitted ruefully, 'I don't like myself too much, either. I can only put it down to body chemicals—ours must be too volatile to mix comfortably.'

'That's one way of putting it,' he muttered, looking unconvinced.

'What other way is there?' she asked. 'The plain fact is we went too far too fast, and I shouldn't think that's normal for either of us. Something had to go wrong.'

'Don't you know what?' he asked, looking thunderstruck.

'No,' she sighed, remembering wistfully how she'd thought his fingers had trembled when he'd cupped her face in his hands, beguiling her into believing for a precious fraction of time that his emotions had been as deep and true as her own.

Tobias came away from the window and sat moodily on the edge of the bed, directly opposite her. 'You made me lose my temper. You shouldn't have smiled like that.'

Felice shook her head, mystified. 'How did I smile?'

'Like the cat that's swallowed the cream. That smile said it all.'

'Said what?' she asked, more mystified than ever.

'That you thought I was as easy a target as my great-uncle. All those years of not paying any rent! Did you really expect me to believe it was because he chose to ignore the fact that you were living in the cottage?'

Felice had been expecting some kind of attack—but not from this angle. Stung by its unfairness, she exclaimed, 'It's the truth! I'm not responsible for the way Old Josh was.'

'You're responsible for taking advantage of his senility,' Tobias tossed back at her, 'and ever since we've met you've been working on the best way of taking advantage of me, too. Exactly when did you decide that flat on your back was the most appropriate?'

'How dare you?' she gasped. 'If I were that sort of a woman, I wouldn't have stopped just now, would I?'

'Of course you would. Stupidity isn't one of your faults, and you'd have to be stupid to go all the way without first making sure you'd get what you wanted from me.'

Felice jumped to her feet, her eyes blazing with fury. 'You've got me all wrong. Old Josh was eccentric, not senile, and I've already told you it was never my intention to take advantage of him. He created the situation I'm in over the cottage, not me. And as for you——'

She broke off, biting her lip.

'Go on,' Tobias encouraged her with a sardonic smile. 'Next you should be denying that you intended to take advantage of me.'

Felice's face flamed. 'I can't, and you know it.'

'Yes, I know it.'

Momentarily, she thought Tobias sounded as disappointed and disillusioned as she was herself, but she decided that must be something else she was imagining. 'At least I was honest,' she defended herself. 'I made it plain I wanted a lease for the cottage, but I hoped to talk you into it. *Talk*, Tobias,' she stressed. 'I'd never have used my body to get it.'

'I'm sure you wouldn't,' he agreed softly. 'Your magnificent body is worth far more than that. The cottage was only a gambit. It's the Hall you're really after. You soon made that obvious enough.'

Felice gasped, 'You're mad! Mad in a way Old Josh never was!'

'On the contrary, I'm depressingly sane. Give me credit for knowing when a woman's making a dead set at me, particularly when she's already been warned against it. Heaven knows I wanted to believe you were different. I even gave you a last chance to prove that you were when I kissed you, but you muffed it. That smile of yours was just that little bit too triumphant. No man likes to be used too blatantly, least of all me.'

Felice breathed wonderingly, 'What makes you think you're so marvellous that women want to throw themselves at you?'

'Oh, not at me,' he answered drily. 'At what I can give them.'

'And that's what you think I've done?' she went on, flabbergasted. 'Let me get this straight. You think all women are gold-diggers, is that it? Including me?'

Tobias got up and went back to the window, leaning his elbows on the deep embrasure as he stared moodily over the frost-covered meadows to the sea. 'I don't go in for name-calling, Felice. It's outdated and it isn't necessary, anyway. Let's just say women have a way of letting me know if they're available. After that, it's just a matter of agreeing terms.'

Rigid with outrage, she demanded, 'And you think my terms are the Hall?'

'You're the one who advocated plain speaking on the grounds that it saves a lot of time,' he reminded her. 'I don't know why you're in such a huff because I've taken you at your word. Nor do I know why you threw out all those sexual signals if you didn't expect me to call your bluff. I thought that was what you wanted.'

'Wh-what *I* wanted!' she stammered, disbelieving. 'I don't believe I'm hearing this! I loathe being treated as just a body. It's not my fault if I'm built in a way that puts only one thought in men's minds.'

'It's not a fault, it's a delight,' Tobias contradicted, turning to face her and hunching his powerful shoulders against the wall, 'but you can't have it all ways. If you want to be wooed leisurely with chocolates and flowers you shouldn't have come on to me so strongly.'

'I didn't!' she exclaimed, her voice almost snapping with exasperation. 'I was just being friendly.'

'If you want to avoid similar mistakes in the future, try to be less friendly and more exclusive,' he advised her smoothly.

Felice gasped again, then realised she couldn't explain why she'd been particularly friendly to him—without confessing how deeply she'd been attracted to him! She'd rather be misunderstood than do that!

She seethed with impotent fury, but she was wounded, too. Tobias's cynicism had cut her deeply, partly because of the injustice of it, but mostly because it ridiculed everything that had made her warm to him in the first place.

'Then here's where I start being more exclusive,' she
said between gritted teeth, turning pointedly away from
him and stalking out of the room. Once in the panelled
passage she kept on going, down the beautiful staircase,
out of the castle wing and into the splendid Indian hall.

She could hear his footsteps behind her, echoing positively around the old building, and closing on her fast.
The temptation to run from him was almost overpowering, but she kept her head high, her back straight, and
her strides steady. Contempt was what he deserved, and
contempt was what he would get.

At last she reached the front door and gratefully she
stretched for the handle. She needed desperately to escape
this fantasy world and get outside into reality, where
crazy, unbelievable things didn't happen. Then, perhaps,
she would be able to shut down the turbulent emotions
Tobias had unleashed in her.

But how dared he think such awful things about her?
How dared he? All right, so she'd been unguarded, but
only because her instincts told her she didn't have to be
on her guard with Tobias.

So much for instincts!

Swaying between rage, hurt and a desolating feeling
of betrayal, she froze when Tobias's arm reached past
her. His strong hand closed over hers, trapping it on the
handle, preventing her escape into the outside world.

She couldn't bring herself to swing round to face him,
so she remained rigidly as she was. Tobias put his other
arm around her waist and pulled her back against him.
Unwillingly, Felice experienced once more the shock and
delight of feeling her body pressed against his.

The dubious pleasure turned swiftly to indignation
when he bent his head and kissed her ear as a lover might.
'Felice,' he murmured, his breath tantalising her ear and

all her senses, 'I never meant to offend you by being too frank, but I was only following your lead, remember?'

Felice chose not to remember anything, nor to say anything, either. She was too busy trying to suppress the excitement that the closeness of his body communicated to hers. She thought despairingly that this instant arousal of her senses was another kind of betrayal, melting her anger as it did, beguiling her brain...

Oh, grief, what was happening to her? What *had* happened to her ever since she'd set eyes on Tobias Hunter? It couldn't be love, because love needed certain things to grow, things he knew nothing about.

What did that leave? Lust, she thought, then all her thoughts splintered into confusion as Tobias drew her closer still and continued, 'A situation like this won't go away by our ignoring it. We have to resolve it in a way that will be acceptable to both of us. It's the only sensible thing to do.'

'I don't know what you mean,' she retorted frigidly.

'Yes, you do,' he challenged. 'Something happened between us when we met, something so positive there was an almost audible click. We might be mad at each other right now, and the chances are we'll be mad at each other again, but there's no running away from a feeling this powerful. There won't be any peace for either of us until we're together.'

Felice shivered because every word he said rang with truth, but it was an unacceptable truth—unacceptable to her, anyway. She wasn't like him. She couldn't settle for the best deal she could get, not when it was so much less than she needed to make her happy.

Respect, love, trust. Those were the things she needed, however much her wilful body might betray her.

Tobias's warm breath on her ear again tormented her senses as he went on softly, 'We're both realists, so let's talk about it.'

It was at that moment Felice discovered she wasn't a realist at all. She was a romantic—a hopeless romantic. Her busy life, her practical outlook, her managing ways...all had been a massive cover-up for the emptiness within her, an emptiness she'd been unaware of until Tobias had exposed it.

The irony was that, having exposed it, he could only offer her realism, and not the romance she craved.

Something seemed to wither within her, and it took all her courage to turn within his encircling arm to face him. 'This talk—it would be about an affair, wouldn't it?' she asked with difficulty. 'That's what you mean when you keep talking about terms?'

'Of course.' He seemed surprised she should have doubted it. 'We want each other, and you also want the Hall. You can have it in return for being my mistress for as long as it amuses us both. That will be your only claim on me when we part, but naturally I'll have a legal agreement drawn up to protect both our interests.'

Good heavens, Felice thought, the last of her illusions dying. He sounded so businesslike he might have been negotiating for a car or a yacht—or anything that might have taken his fancy. Didn't he realise she was flesh and blood, with all that that entailed?

Feelings, for a start...

'You don't believe in wasting time, do you?' she managed, when she came out of shock.

'You're not exactly a slowcoach yourself.'

Had she seemed that way? Had she really? It didn't seem possible—any more possible than this 'deal' he was setting up. She shook her head in disbelief and whispered, 'I can't believe you're serious.'

'What's the matter? I've got your terms right, haven't I?'

'You haven't got anything right,' she told him sadly. 'About me—about anything. If you had, you'd know that, even to contemplate what you're suggesting, I'd want so much more than the Hall.'

His eyebrows rose. 'Ravishing as you are, you can hardly suppose you're worth the entire estate! I'm generous, Felice, but I stop short of being foolhardy.'

Damn the man, he'd wilfully misunderstood her again! She couldn't explain, either, not without letting him know that feelings came first, second and last with her. And what a humiliating waste of time that would be, when the only feeling he understood was lust!

Outrage kept her silent, but he misinterpreted that, too. 'My God,' he breathed, 'you're holding out for marriage.'

'No!' Felice denied hotly, her cheeks burning with embarrassment, but Tobias was releasing her and beginning to laugh. Rich, genuine laughter that echoed around the domed hall and returned to mock her.

'Stop it!' she said fiercely. 'Stop it!'

'I'm trying,' he said, smiling at her with a candour that would have tugged at her heart-strings if only she hadn't been the victim of his amusement. 'You should have done your research on me a bit more thoroughly, Felice. Then you'd have known why I always take mistresses, and never wives. Mistresses are more amusing, and a great deal less expensive in the long run.'

Once more his cynicism appalled her, and she scoffed, 'Love on the cheap!'

His amusement faded and he asked scornfully, 'Who said anything about love? I wouldn't call my offer of the Hall exactly cheap, either.'

'Everything about you is cheap,' she retorted. 'Cheap because you see everything in terms of money!'

'I'd have to be blind not to see you put too high a price on yourself,' he snapped back.

Felice gave up. They were arguing from different standpoints and getting farther and farther apart all the time. He believed what he wanted to believe, and that was it! Nothing she said was going to change him.

She drew herself up to her full height and replied disdainfully, 'I'm only for hire as a taxi driver, Mr Hunter. If you're no longer interested in that, I'll be on my way.'

She didn't wait for an answer, but wrenched open the door and left him. She stormed down the drive a lot faster than she'd walked up it, her mind a shifting kaleidoscope of impressions that wouldn't settle into in one clear picture or one uncomplicated emotion. It was all a hopeless jumble. Tobias, if nothing else, had certainly screwed up her head. Or was it her heart?

Oh, hell!

Exasperated, she left the driveway and detoured through the trees to get over the high wall, trying to convince herself that Tobias had somehow got mixed up with her lifelong fascination for the Hall. Once she got them separated in her mind, she'd be all right again.

She breathed a bit more easily when she dropped on to the grass verge outside the wall, but she almost stopped breathing altogether when she reached her car and found Tobias already sitting in it.

He must have climbed over the gate, but then he wouldn't have to worry about doing any damage, would he? He owned the place, although from his attitude he might also have owned the whole of the world and everyone in it.

But now me, she vowed. Never me.

She toyed with the idea of ordering him out, but it was an order she'd never be able to enforce if he resisted. Besides, the quickest way of getting rid of him was by taking him wherever he wanted to go. She climbed into the driver's seat and asked formally, 'Where to?'

'The airstrip. I have a lunch date in London.'

She was startled. A lunch date? That meant he'd only set aside the smallest possible time to look over his inheritance, so he'd never really been interested in it at all. Whatever had happened—or might have happened—between them, in the long run she'd always been wasting her time. He was as impervious to the magic of Woodlands as he was to the magic of love.

She was so rattled to find herself again thinking of love and Tobias at one and the same time that she crashed the gears twice as she turned the car. Damn! What was it about him that made all her normal skills desert her?

When the car was finally facing the right way, she put her foot down hard on the accelerator and speeded back to the airfield. They were almost there before she realised her clumsiness was due to her still being extraordinarily sensitive to his presence.

An annoyed frown settled on her normally sunny face and Tobias, turning in his seat to watch her, said, 'You're sulking. I hate women who sulk.'

'That suits me,' she retorted stonily.

'You know what your problem is, Felice? You enjoy cutting off your nose to spite your face.'

'I won't bother telling you what your problem is. It would take all day,' she snapped back, and drove through the gates of the airfield fuming.

When she stopped, Tobias looked at the meter and wasted no time in paying her or getting out of the car. 'Definitely sulking,' he reaffirmed. Then he slammed the car door on her and walked purposefully towards his aircraft.

Felice watched him for a few moments, her irritation fading into a poignancy that almost made her want to weep as she remembered how very differently she'd felt when Tobias had walked towards her earlier that morning. Everything had seemed possible then, and now nothing was.

She felt a different girl from the one who'd driven out so confidently to meet him, but she blamed herself for that. Hadn't she suspected he was a sleeping tiger long before she'd actually been mauled?

Reaction to her fancifulness set in, and her lips curved in wry self-mockery. All that had really happened, she scolded herself, was that she'd fallen foul of a predatory male who happened to think he was God's gift to women, and for once she hadn't been able to cope.

Well, there was no need to make a major drama out of it. Everybody came unstuck sometimes, and this...sadness that was making her feel so low right now would soon pass.

Her eyes were bleak, though, and her soft lips drooped wistfully as she did a U-turn and drove back on to the road. She didn't look back when the peace of the Sunday-drowsy valley was shattered by the sound of a plane revving to life.

She didn't want to watch Tobias fly out of her life as abruptly as he'd flown into it. For some peculiar reason, she wasn't half as glad about it as she should have been.

As the days passed, Felice waited to bounce back to her normal ebullient self. Somehow, though, she never quite managed to bounce through the cloud of gloom that was hanging over her.

It began to dawn on her that the joy she usually brought to her everyday living was gone, stolen by an impossible man who outraged everything that was straight and true and decent about her. Unfortunately, that didn't stop her pining for him.

He dominated her thoughts and dreams, reminding her forcibly of his assertion that there wouldn't be any peace for either of them until they were together.

Every time she remembered it, she ground her teeth with rage, and in her stronger moments she even managed to convince herself she wasn't pining at all— but merely waiting for Tobias to enforce the eviction order. By trying so hard to charm a legal tenancy out of him, she was sure she'd achieved the very opposite.

So, all in all, she faced each day without enthusiasm, getting through her work with a forced cheerfulness that fooled everybody except herself. But since everybody was used to her being cheerful, they didn't take much fooling.

When she'd dropped out of college, she'd set herself up as a landscape gardener, and, after a precarious start, her business had expanded gradually by word-of-mouth recommendation.

Now she tended large gardens as well as small, and her white van emblazoned with the legend 'Lawson Gardening Services' was familiar in the nearby village of Bixley, and in several other villages as well.

During spring and summer when she was rushed off her feet she hired extra workers, but February was the last of the winter 'dead' months and she could cope easily alone. Too easily sometimes, which was why she worked weekends as a taxi driver to keep her income up.

On the Wednesday after her traumatic meeting with Tobias, she stopped off at the newsagents in Bixley to get the local weekly paper before driving on to the cottage for lunch. The sooner she started house-hunting again, the better. It wasn't a cheerful prospect, and her spirits were at an all-time low as she parked beside the cottage and let her two black and white collies out of the back of the van.

She always took the dogs with her on her gardening jobs. They were well trained and her customers saved titbits for them. Sometimes she felt more of a mobile bone disposal unit than a gardener.

Out of the blue, she found herself wondering whether Tobias liked dogs...

Why, oh, why did everything she did or even thought have to return to him? Grimacing, she took the dogs into the kitchen at the back of the house and made some cheese on toast. While she ate it, she scanned the short column of rented accommodation in the paper, and found her pessimism well-founded. Plenty of furnished accommodation, particularly short-term winter lets, but nothing remotely suitable for her.

Felice looked at her watch and decided to put her feet up for half an hour before she set out on her next job. She went into the passage and saw that some letters had been delivered after she'd left that morning.

She picked them up and wandered into the sitting-room, switching on the gas fire and shifting a cat so she could sink into her favourite armchair. The cat promptly jumped on to her lap and she stroked it absently as she sifted through the mail. It was all junk, except for one white envelope embossed with the name of a London firm of solicitors.

She really didn't want to open that letter, so certain was she that the axe hanging over her head since Old Josh had died was about to fall, the last supporting thread cut by Tobias. She chewed her lip in dismay and looked around her.

Every room in the cottage was crammed with the sentimental clutter of her family's lifetime...books, photographs, paintings, ornaments, knick-knacks and goodness knew what else. The attics were crammed with hockey sticks, tennis rackets, toys and all sorts of oddments that were too precious to some member of the family to be thrown away.

Tobias knew nothing of this, hadn't wanted to know. In fairness, there was no reason for him to care anyway, except that if their positions had been reversed she'd have cared.

Tobias, though, had made it crystal clear he cared for nobody but himself. It was the difference between them, and, the more she considered it, the more insuperable the difference became.

Felice turned the letter over and over in her hands, then finally plucked up the courage to rip it open. Sure enough, a frightening-looking legal document fell into her lap. She unfolded it, scanned it quickly, then stared unseeing into space.

She couldn't believe it. It was a two-year lease for the cottage and the authorising signature at the bottom was Tobias's own.

Her fingers shook slightly as she traced his name, willing the bold strokes to tell her why he'd done this. He'd wanted her. She'd refused him. He wasn't magnanimous in defeat. So why?

CHAPTER SIX

THE sudden shrill of the telephone interrupted Felice's thoughts, and it wasn't an interruption she appreciated. She had some hard thinking to do. Really hard thinking.

'Felice?' an exasperated voice asked. 'At last! I've been trying to get you all morning. It's Charles,' the caller added belatedly.

Felice's eyebrows went up as she wondered, What now? Charles Martin had recently taken over his father's estate agency in Bixley and she couldn't imagine what he was exasperated about. She was about to enquire when he went on, 'Felice, are you there?'

'No, this is just my wraith,' she replied, feeling exasperated herself. Charles was a few years older than herself but they'd more or less grown up together, so there was no need to stand on ceremony with him. 'What bee's buzzing around in your bonnet? It isn't like you to lose your cool.'

'You won't be so cool yourself when you hear my news. Tobias Hunter has turned up—Old Josh's great-nephew!'

'Turned up where?' Felice asked, her nervous system going into overdrive at the very thought of Tobias being in her vicinity.

'I don't mean literally, although I gather he's been down to Woodlands to give it the once over.'

'I know,' Felice replied, her alarm vanishing. 'He made a quick inspection on Sunday. I drove him from the air-strip to the Hall.'

'You might have told me,' Charles grumbled. 'What sort of a man is he?'

'Oh, the usual, as far as I could tell,' Felice replied airily. 'You know, two arms, two legs and a head.' She wasn't about to go into raptures over exactly how excitingly Tobias's anatomy was put together.

'Is he anything like Old Josh?'

'Don't ask me, I was only the taxi driver,' she hedged. 'What's it to do with you, anyway? You're not professionally involved with the Hall, are you?'

'From this morning, yes. Mr Hunter's solicitors have appointed me his local agent.'

Then Tobias was selling. Felice didn't understand the disappointment surging through her. It wasn't exactly a surprise. She tried to stay chirpy as she replied, 'Congratulations, but what's it to do with me?'

'Everything, my girl,' Charles replied importantly. 'That's why I need to talk to you. Can you drop by the office this afternoon?'

Felice was puzzled but was too wary to show it. 'We're talking now,' she pointed out.

'Yes, but I hardly ever see you these days, and this is definitely worth a face-to-face. Until this afternoon, then.' He hung up before she could argue.

Felice replaced the phone thoughtfully. It wasn't like Charles to be cryptic or assertive, not with her, anyway. She dated him occasionally, but, although he was good-looking in his way, she'd never been really attracted to him.

A pity she couldn't say the same about Tobias!

Sighing, she whizzed around getting ready to go out again. Charles had dangled just the right carrot to get her into his office without any loss of time. She desperately needed to know what Tobias was up to. It might shed some light on why he'd so unexpectedly granted her the lease.

She'd have to be cautious, though. Charles was a name-dropper and a gossip, loving to give the impression he was on the inside of everything that went on in the neighbourhood. If he got an inkling that anything unusual had occurred between her and Tobias, it would be all round the village by morning.

That wouldn't bother Tobias, of course. For one thing he was too arrogant to care, and for another he wouldn't be around even to hear it. But she would, and it would bother her. She had to live here.

Sitting in Charles's office fifteen minutes later, she was discovering how difficult it was for an outgoing person like herself to be secretive without that causing comment in itself. 'Oh, come on, Felice,' Charles was saying sceptically, 'I'm sure you know more about Mr Hunter than you're letting on. He must have made some sort of impression on you.'

Felice's harassed mind whirled with impressions. The strength of Tobias's arms, the fire of his lips, the fury of his anger, the short-lived belief they were two of a kind and therefore made for each other...

But all these impressions were female and emotional, and for Charles's benefit she had to try to see Tobias as another man would. Not the easiest task in the world.

'He seems used to getting his own way.' That seemed a safe enough thing to say, but Charles looked so dissatisfied that she enlarged, 'Inheriting Woodlands didn't appear to mean much to him, so he can't be hard up for a penny or two.'

'Hard up for a penny or two?' Charles echoed in amazement. 'Haven't you made the connection?'

'What connection?' she asked blankly.

'He's the publishing tycoon. The T.B. Hunter of T.B. Hunter Consolidated Press! His media empire covers everything from newspapers and magazines to TV stations. Compared to all that, the Woodlands Estate is no more than a flea on an elephant's back.'

'It's the sort of flea I wouldn't mind scratching.' Felice tried to speak whimsically but her voice was hollow. With all that wealth and power, no wonder Tobias was used to women throwing themselves at him. His cynicism didn't stem from vanity, then, but from experience, as he'd maintained—but she still couldn't forgive him for lumping her in with all the rest of the women who pestered him.

He should have *known* she was different. She wasn't clear how, but he should have known, anyway!

'What are you looking so thoughtful about?' Charles asked suspiciously.

'Me? Oh, I—er—was just wondering what the "B" in T.B. Hunter stands for,' she improvised.

'Bertram. I've been doing a bit of research on him since I found out exactly who he is,' Charles explained. 'It was his father's name.'

A reminiscent smile she couldn't quite control curved Felice's lips. 'Tobias doesn't look like a Bertie. Anything but.'

'Why should you say that? Did anything happen between you two?' Charles asked, a speculative gleam lighting his greenish eyes.

Felice narrowly avoided blushing the colour of his red hair. 'Heavens, no,' she denied swiftly. 'It's just that Bertie doesn't seem the right sort of name for a Press baron. I mean, they're not exactly pussycats, are they?'

'Felice, you should be more respectful towards T.B. Hunter,' Charles chided her pompously. 'He's an extremely powerful man.'

In more ways than you know, she thought, but Charles was going on, 'His main base is in Canada but he has homes in other parts of the world, including London. It's our good fortune that he intends to use the Hall for weekends when he's in the UK.'

'Use it?' Felice exclaimed, completely taken by surprise. 'You mean he isn't selling?'

'No, and that's good for the village. A man with his resources will provide a lot of local employment—certainly more than Old Josh ever did, with his weird reclusive ways. Frankly, I thought the Hall would go the same road as of a lot of other big houses and be carved up into flats.'

Felice, astutely cutting through Charles's pomposity, knew that what he was really pleased about was getting a slice of the action. She kept her peace, though, because the implications of Tobias living at Woodlands was hitting her, blowing every other consideration from her mind.

Could it be Tobias's businesslike brain had slapped her in some mental file labelled 'unfinished business', and this was his way of keeping her close until he got the result he wanted? After all, there'd been enough conviction in his voice when he'd said there wouldn't be any peace for either of them until they were together.

Did he still, in spite of everything, feel that way?

A tiny shiver touched Felice's spine, and she winced with shame because it wasn't entirely unpleasurable. Then her eyes widened with amazement as Charles asked, 'How do you feel about working for Mr Hunter?'

'*Me*? You mean he needs a permanent chauffeur?'

'No,' Charles replied with a touch of impatience. 'Mr Hunter wants the gardens at the Hall redesigned and put in order.'

'But I didn't tell him I'm a landscape gardener. How could he possibly know?'

'He doesn't,' Charles replied, even more impatiently. 'What's the matter with you today? It's entirely up to me whom I hire on his behalf.'

'Oh, I see! He doesn't know you're hiring me, then?' She could relax. This obviously wasn't a dastardly plot on Tobias's part to get her in his clutches.

'Is there any reason why he should?' Charles demanded.

'No,' she replied lamely.

'Then what are you making all the fuss about?'

'I'm not. It just that he might—er—find it a bit odd that I have two jobs, that's all,' she improvised.

'Really, Felice, if this is your way of saying the job's too big for you, just come right out with it. I thought you'd be glad of a lucrative contract at this time of year.'

He was right. Normally she'd have jumped at the chance of such a big job, and working on the gardens of her beloved Woodlands would have had the added attraction of being a labour of love! But——

'Where is Tobias now?' she asked.

'Tobias?' Charles stared at her. 'Are you on first-name terms?'

Felice could have bitten off her tongue. 'He's a Canadian, not at all formal,' she waffled. 'Mind you, having a lady taxi driver probably took him by surprise and lowered his reserve. It—er—often happens with male passengers.'

'You made it sound as though you were friends,' Charles accused.

'No, we're definitely not that,' she replied, this time with enough conviction to lull his suspicions. 'Do you know where he is at the moment?'

'I understand he's returned to Canada for a month. He wants the gardens sorted out while he's away. Can you round up enough casual labour to get the work done in that time, plus keep up with your normal commitments?'

'Yes.'

'Then you'll do it?'

Felice hesitated only fractionally. Then once more she said, 'Yes.' After all, with Tobias safely out of the way, there wasn't a single reason why she should refuse. The decision made, she stood up. 'Thanks, Charles, for putting the work my way.'

He smiled at her. 'Thank me properly by letting me take you to the country-club dance at the end of the month.'

'Mine will be a family party. The twins and Janetta will be home for half-term, so unless you fancy ferrying all of us...?'

'It's not what I wanted, but, if that's the only way I can get you, all right,' he grumbled.

Felice gave him her first real smile of the day. 'That's what I like about you, Charles,' she murmured. 'You're always so gracious.' Then she whisked herself out of his office before he had time to think of a suitable reply.

She only had one gardening job that afternoon, and normally she'd have used her spare time to catch up on her shopping and domestic chores. But this was no longer a normal afternoon.

At half-past two she was pacing the grounds of Woodlands Hall, her collies at her heels as she made copious notes of work that needed doing. Later on she could sort them into the right sort of order to get the job done smoothly and quickly.

She started in the walled kitchen garden. It was pitifully neglected, and she decided to restore it herself. She imagined it as it should be, with neat rows of vegetables and fruit to keep the kitchen supplied, and aromatic with the scent of fresh herbs during the growing season.

Her imagination went one further and supplied little children running along the paved paths, playing and laughing, and hopefully having fun without doing too much damage. She could even see their faces, and blinked hard as she realised they all looked like Tobias.

The impression was vivid enough to drive her out of one of the wooden gates set in the rose-coloured brick walls and on to a tour of the formal flowerbeds. There weren't many of them.

Most of the extensive grounds were kept in their natural grass and wooded state, needing little care apart from clearing away seasonal decay. Several severe gales had hit the island over the past weeks, though, and Woodlands had had its share of damage.

As time passed and Felice continued pacing the grounds, her notes growing ever longer, she found that few trees were actually down, although lots of branches had been ripped away or were hanging dangerously from otherwise healthy trees. She would have to sub-contract that sort of work to a tree specialist, and a plentiful supply of logs for the house would be a result of it.

Once more her imagination threw out an unwelcome picture—of Tobias and his mistress of the moment sitting by one of the Hall's many fireplaces, the logs glowing brightly, the rugs at their feet ideal for making love...

She was seared with an envy so sharp that she actually gasped, then she looked around self-consciously to see if anybody had heard her, but of course she was alone. Even the dogs had run off, rabbit-hunting among the wildly overgrown blackberry bushes down by the river.

They would find her again soon enough. The early February dusk was already falling and they would be wanting their supper. So should she, but somehow she'd lost much of her appetite since Sunday, and she wasn't quite finished yet.

She still had to inspect the magnolias planted around a summerhouse designed like a miniature Grecian temple. It was sited on top of a gentle hill so that anybody sitting there could enjoy a panoramic view over the gardens and meadows to the sea.

There was barely enough light left, and she'd have to get a move on or it would be pitch black before she got home. Yet she felt no inclination to hurry. Home was no longer a welcoming place where she could relax after a busy day, appreciating her solitude. Home now seemed loveless, barren.

Like herself without Tobias.

Exasperated, she thrust her notebook and pen in her pocket and tried to think more positively, but it was no use. Her melancholy deepened with the dusk as she approached the classical columns and portico of the little temple, gleaming ghostly white in the greying landscape.

The trees behind it were rapidly darkening into a shapeless mass against the sky. Felice knew she'd run out of time, and that the magnolias would have to be inspected another day. Still she walked on to the temple, though, drawn by a force more powerful than reason.

Perhaps she would find some kind of peace there that would drive away her depression. She wasn't a melancholic person, never had been, and she didn't know how to cope with a mood like this one. It was as though she

was reaching out for something, and was desolate to the
point of heartbreak because what she sought was beyond
her reach.

'Felice.'

The drawling voice that so delighted and dismayed her
came from nowhere, a sigh on the evening breeze, and
she stopped, poised for flight, looking this way and that.
Her heart was beating so rapidly that she could scarcely
breathe, but when nothing moved she decided the sheer
intensity of her yearning had played a diabolical trick
on her.

She must be so wilfully and wretchedly obsessed with
Tobias that her imagination had again conjured him up
for her. It was eerie, and she joked to herself that any
more of this kind of nonsense and men in white coats
would be coming for her with a strait-jacket!

'Trespassing again?' that well-remembered deep and
sensual voice asked.

It was Tobias! He was no trick of her fevered imagination. He was really here…somewhere. But where?
Then she saw him materialising out of the shadows at
the back of the temple. She couldn't quite suppress a
gasp as she was seared with the pain, the pleasure, and
the uncertainty of once more being close to him.

'I asked if you were trespassing again,' he repeated.

'Caught bang to rights,' she replied, determinedly
making light of it although her heart was hammering so
hard that she thought her ribcage would burst.

But her mind was racing to catch up with the situation, and all the messages it flung out were cautious.
Tobias had no idea she was here legitimately to assess
the state of the gardens, and she had no intention of
telling him.

If she couldn't work on them anonymously, then she wouldn't work on them at all. Otherwise Tobias might think she was deliberately throwing herself his way again, perhaps hoping for a better offer than he'd made her last time.

The only better offer, of course, was marriage. The remembered humiliation of when he'd wrongly jumped to that conclusion himself made her cheeks burn so fiercely that she was profoundly grateful for the masking twilight. Much, much better to let him go on thinking she was trespassing.

She cleared her throat and the little sound was magnified by the intense silence of descending night, signalling to him a nervousness she was trying desperately to hide. Gosh, now she'd have to say something, however inane, just to appear natural. 'I thought you were in Canada,' she managed at last.

'How did you hear that?'

'Oh, native tom-toms,' she replied carelessly.

Tobias was leaning against one of the classical columns supporting the little temple's portico, his arms folded, as relaxed as she was tense. 'The tom-toms got the timing wrong,' he said. 'I don't fly to Canada until tomorrow, but, to get back to the point, how are trespassers punished in these parts, Felice?'

She felt the sensitive hairs at the nape of her neck rise but she replied with a good assumption of unconcern, 'Usually they're let off with a few harsh words and a caution, something you're good at if my memory serves me rightly.'

'There's nothing wrong with your memory, but is it punishment enough for a girl who never learns?'

Tobias eased himself away from the pillar and came deliberately towards her. Felice quivered with a thrill that wasn't quite alarm. Well, yes, alarm, but it was heavily laced with something else. Anticipation. She was waiting, the very stillness of the evening was waiting, for what he would do next.

She lifted her chin defiantly and stood her ground. After all, whatever Tobias took it into his mind to do, she'd already discovered there was a point beyond which he wouldn't go.

Wasn't there? Her confidence ebbed but she couldn't—wouldn't!—back down now. She was much too proud.

'You know, Felice,' Tobias murmured, 'you really shouldn't raise your chin at me like that. Given the sort of man I am, it makes only one punishment possible.'

His big hands grasped her shoulders and she felt the shock and delight of being pulled roughly against his hard body. Her gasp was smothered by his lips coming down on hers with ruthless intent. He wilfully, deliberately, kissed her into panting submission, and then he let her go.

'How would you rate that, Felice?' he asked mockingly. 'Punishment or reward?'

'You—you——' she gasped ineffectually, drawing the back of her hand over her lips as though to wipe away the taste and temptation of him for ever.

'Take it as a lesson never to trespass unprotected on my land after dark. I could have been any man, and you'd have been just as helpless.'

'Any man would have been preferable to you,' she flung at him, 'and this land was perfectly safe until you came here. Besides, I'm not unprotected! I have my dogs with me!'

'I don't see any dogs.'

'They're down by the river chasing rabbits. They'd be here in a flash if I whistled them.'

'Then why didn't you whistle them?'

Felice saw too late the trap she'd fallen into. She could scarcely confess that, mesmerised by his powerful effect on her as usual, she'd forgotten all about the dogs. A very Freudian oversight.

Tobias came to the same conclusion. 'You didn't want to be protected,' he breathed, and swept her back into his arms. His lips sought and claimed hers with a triumph she couldn't deny, and yet she was more frightened than she had ever been before.

This wasn't brutality. It was an act of possession. Tobias was confident now that she was his for the taking. And she wasn't. She wasn't!

She was powerless against his strength so she had to find some other way to fight free, and yet it was so very difficult to think of anything with her mind and senses reeling under the onslaught of his passion.

Her passion.

Oh, grief!

It was at that moment Tobias raised his head to look at her, giving her vital moments to recover some shreds of self-possession. She couldn't bear him to think she was won so cheaply and easily, and so she said, 'If I'm supposed to be showing suitable gratitude for the lease on the cottage, I'd rather you raised the rent.'

She had, it seemed, hit on just the right thing to stop Tobias dead in his tracks. He flung her away from him and ground out, 'You bitch! I didn't issue that lease to put you under obligation to me.'

'Then why did you?' she cried. 'And why are you coming to live here if you hate the place? It doesn't make sense—unless you can't bear the thought of a woman rejecting you, so you have to keep on trying!'

There, she'd said it, put into words the doubts and distrust that had bedevilled her since she'd opened his solicitor's letter and the lease had fallen into her lap.

Tobias said pithily, 'I made a point of reading the inspection report on the cottage made by my great-uncle's executors after his death. It confirmed what you'd told me, that the cottage had been restored to the highest possible order, and kept in that condition. Since there was no record in my great-uncle's accounts that he'd borne the cost, I decided you deserved the lease.'

'Oh,' Felice said, feeling a little foolish.   .

'Yes, "oh",' he mimicked angrily, 'and, as for my decision to keep the Hall, you can blame yourself for that.'

'Me?' she asked uncomprehendingly.

'Yes, you. I'm thirty-six years old and it's time I was thinking about the next generation. Woodlands Hall might not be to my taste, but you were right about its being a great place to raise children. I'm keeping it for that purpose.'

'*Purpose*?' she echoed. 'But—but—children aren't a *purpose*! They're a result of love.'

'They are, or should be, a result of a contract between two people who are attracted to each other, and it doesn't have to be a marriage contract. A business one can give children the same protection. In fact, it can give them even more, since it can't be nullified as easily as a marriage contract can.'

'A marriage isn't a contract,' Felice gasped, horrified. 'It's an exchange of sacred vows between two people in love.'

Tobias laughed sceptically. 'When did you last read the divorce statistics? I'm one of them, and I don't intend to ever be one again.'

So he'd been married, and unhappily by the sound of things. It explained a lot—but not enough! Felice said forthrightly, 'Whatever's happened to you in the past, you can't let it embitter your future. Not if you intend to have children! It wouldn't be fair. It wouldn't even be *decent*!'

'It's realistic, which is more to the point, and if only you could overcome your woolly-headed notions of marriage you'd admit it.'

'Woolly-headed?' she objected fiercely. 'I'm not woolly-headed!'

'Yes, you are. Face facts, Felice. You are as attracted to me as I am to you and——'

'No!' she broke in hotly. 'No!'

'Yes,' he continued inexorably. 'Every time we touch proves that beyond any denial. It's biological, and I can only suppose it's because we met at a time when we both have different needs to be expressed. Mine is for children, and yours is for the Hall. It makes sense to merge those needs into a mutually beneficial relationship that will result in children for me and the Hall for you. All nice and neat and legally tied up so that there are no nasty shocks for either of us at the end of it.'

'No,' Felice whispered, aghast. 'No!'

'You'd say yes fast enough if I deceived you with a lot of piffling love-talk,' he retorted. 'I'm doing you the honour of being honest with you, offering you a steady relationship without the drawbacks of deception and disillusion. We will both know precisely where we stand with each other at all times and, believe me, in the long run that beats anything as transitory as so-called love.'

Felice knew he was cynical, but she couldn't believe he was as coldly calculating as this. Revulsion made her cry, 'That isn't an honour. It's disgusting!'

'Still holding out for marriage, Felice?' he mocked. 'Well, I'm afraid you're overrating your power over me again. I'm interested, but I could just as soon get interested in somebody else. Somebody who will have and raise my children on my terms.'

'Then go and find her! I'll admit I love the Hall, but not enough to take you along with it! And that should prove to you that if anybody's overrating their power here, it's you.'

'I gave you credit for being a sensible woman, Felice, but you're really rather stupid,' he retorted harshly. 'Haven't you learned yet not to cut off your nose to spite your face?'

'My nose, my face,' she retorted angrily. She was doubly angry to find how childish she sounded even to her own ears, and that goaded her to add, 'I'll never be your mistress, Tobias Hunter. Attracted to you, huh! I don't even like you!'

There was another silence, and somehow Tobias always seemed even more dangerous when he was silent than when he was saying something. Her nerves cringed as he warned ominously, 'The temptation to prove you a liar is almost irresistible, Felice, so you've never needed protection quite as much as you do at this moment. You'd better whistle for your dogs.'

Felice didn't argue. She whistled.

CHAPTER SEVEN

THE dogs came hurtling out of the darkness and flung themselves joyfully at Felice as though they hadn't seen her for a week. She made a fuss of them, then called them to order. They sat obediently, tongues lolling, the white fur on their faces and ruffs distinctive in the darkness, showing their collie breed.

'So that's your protection,' Tobias said, looking them over. 'They're not exactly slavering Rottweilers, are they?'

'They'd give anybody a hard time, if necessary,' she replied crossly, thinking that Tobias was very shrewd. There was no hint of aggression in his voice now, nothing to make the dogs react with hostility to him.

In fact, when he clicked his fingers they went willingly to him, and fussed around him as though he were a lifelong friend. The traitors, she thought, but she wasn't surprised. She wasn't proof against Tobias's charm herself, in those rare moments when he chose to warm her with it.

Only remembered moments now, she thought wistfully, almost envious of the dogs as Tobias's strong hands alternately ruffled and smoothed their silky coats. She said involuntarily, 'You can't be all bad, not if the dogs like you.'

He straightened up, and, although it was too dark to read his expression, she thought he sounded regretful as he said, 'Unfortunately, you seem to have an uncanny ability to bring out the worst in me. When I'm with you,

I find myself saying and doing things I never intended to.'

Felice's pulses leapt with hope as she sensed he was coming as close to lowering his guard as it was possible for him to. It was on the tip of her tongue to confess, That's the way you affect me, too, when he went on, 'If only you could face up to facts, I reckon we'd have a lot going for us.'

'Everything's what you reckon, isn't it?' she replied sadly, feeling that the moment to re-establish rapport with him had come and gone before she could do anything about it. 'What I reckon doesn't count.'

'It might, if you cared to persuade me.'

His voice was soft, encouraging. Felice's wayward heart began to thump in a painfully erratic way, but she'd lost the courage to lower her own guard. Once more she was afraid of weakening, and exposing herself to his scorn, so she retorted spiritedly, 'Me, persuade you? If ever I'm that hard up, I'll let you know.'

The moment she said it, she regretted it, but it was too late. Tobias snapped, 'That does it! I've finished with wasting my time on you. Don't trip over any more mythical roots on your way off my land——'

'It wasn't a mythical root!' she broke in furiously. 'It was real.'

'—because I won't be there to catch you,' he continued inexorably. 'In fact, I hope you break your damned neck!'

With that, he sheered off into the darkness, leaving her alone. That round to me, she thought, but she felt too forlorn to enjoy her triumph. The dogs were hesitating, looking from Tobias's retreating form to her, as if asking for guidance.

'We've been dumped,' she told them, saying it aloud
in a masochistic need to hurt herself so that she could
forget how much she was already hurting. 'It's what I
wanted and what I've got. And I feel so happy about it
that if I'm very, very lucky I *will* break my damned neck!'

A sketchy night's sleep brought little solace but a lot of
resolution. As soon as her bank opened on Thursday
morning, Felice converted the eight years' saved rent into
a cheque made out to T.B. Hunter, enclosed it with a
brief note of thanks for the lease, and sent it off to
Tobias's solicitors.

There! That should prove to him that she wasn't, and
never had been, a gold-digger. She didn't look too closely
into why she needed to prove anything to him when he
was determined to think the worst of her, anyway. She
just accepted that she needed to.

It took all her resolution not to send his lease back to
him, too. But, for all Tobias believed she couldn't face
up to facts, she knew it would be an unforgivable piece
of self-indulgence to fling away the family home while
her brothers and sister were still dependent on her.

And money was the reason she decided to go ahead
with restoring the gardens at Woodlands. She'd faced a
few financial crises over the years, and, although she'd
managed to survive them, she'd always had the security
of knowing she could draw on the rent if the worst came
to the worst.

Now she had no such security, and the Woodlands
contract would give her a little nest egg if another cash
crisis occurred. All right, so Tobias would be paying her,
but it would be money honestly earned.

The nitty-gritty was that she had to go on being what
she'd learned to be so well—practical—however much

it bruised her spirit and wounded her pride. And, if that
wasn't facing up to unpleasant facts, what was?

With teeth clenched and a determined smile pinned to
her face, she spent the rest of the week reorganising and
delegating her regular work, and recruiting a small army
to work at Woodlands, so that first thing Monday
morning the work was able to begin.

At first Felice, in spite of all her resolution, couldn't
help feeling nervous. Tobias was so unpredictable that
she kept expecting him to step out from behind every
tree. Eventually she settled down, reminding herself she
had his own word for it that he was in Canada.

Besides, if he did return unexpectedly, the worst he
could do was run her off his land. She stood in no danger
of being assaulted, because she'd succeeded so well in
killing off whatever desire he'd had for her.

The tragedy was that she hadn't managed to do the
same efficient job on herself.

Tobias, unfortunately, was very much still with her.
If not in body, then in mind and spirit. She didn't want
to think about her heart. It was numb, and as the days
passed the fact that her integrity was still intact became
less and less of a consolation.

There was relief of a sort on the following Saturday
with the arrival home for half-term of Janetta, fully
eighteen years old now and almost a carbon-copy of
Felice, except that she hadn't grown as tall and
curvaceous.

She shared Felice's affinity for the land and didn't
mind hard work, so as soon as she'd unpacked she joined
Felice in the kitchen garden at Woodlands.

'It's weird being here legitimately,' she confided to
Felice as they dug out rows of cabbages that had gone
to seed. 'I keep expecting to have to make a run for it.'

'I know the feeling,' Felice sympathised. 'Being a trespasser's a lot more fun, but it's still a thrill for me to be working on these gardens.'

Janetta tossed a cabbage on to the heap in a wheelbarrow and said, 'You've always had a special love for Woodlands, haven't you? What's the new owner like? Did you tell me his name?'

'Er—no. It's Tobias. Tobias Hunter.' Felice was glad that exertion had already flushed her cheeks. It was terrible to react like a flustered teenager at the mere mention of his name. It was even more terrible to be less than honest with her sister, but she preferred to lick her wounds in private.

'Tell me about him,' Janetta invited.

'I don't know much, except that he's Canadian, a Press baron, and intends to live here for some part of the year. He's in Canada at the moment and he wants the gardens sorted out by the time he returns. That's in about three weeks.'

Felice had no intention of revealing Tobias's reason for keeping Woodlands, far less the part he'd wanted her to play in it—when he'd still wanted her. She winced as a pang of regret shot through her, and then was angry with herself for feeling any regret at all. Tobias simply wasn't worth it. Why, oh, why did she keep having to tell herself that?

'The twins will pitch in as well,' Janetta replied. 'When are they due home?'

'Next Friday. Their rugby tour overlapped the end of term, and they're spending a few days with Nick Holt— you remember the boy who came to us for Christmas because his parents were abroad?'

'Will I ever forget?' Janetta quipped, grinning. 'Sixteen years old and he fell in love with me! I'd forgotten how intense puppy love could be.'

'You poor old lady!' Felice exclaimed, throwing a muddy cabbage at her. 'You're still at the puppy-love stage yourself.'

'I'm not at any stage,' Janetta retorted, tossing the cabbage back. 'I've got college to get through and a career to launch before I'll have any time for that sort of distraction.'

'Very high-minded of you,' Felice smiled, ending the game by dropping the battered cabbage in the wheelbarrow. Janetta obviously had no idea how much of a 'distraction' love could be. Not that she had much herself. What she felt for Tobias couldn't possibly be love...

She was relieved when Janetta changed the subject by asking, 'Seen anything of our least-favourite cousin lately?'

Felice had no trouble identifying Serena, and as she loosened more cabbages in the soil she replied, 'No, she hasn't been down for ages. She phones occasionally, though, when she gets a particularly good job. One that gets her in the fashion mags or takes her overseas. Or both.'

'Envious?' Janetta asked thoughtfully.

'No,' Felice replied, laughing genuinely for the first time that week. 'I'm a country bumpkin and probably always will be. Her life is my idea of hell, and just as well. I'm built more like a Las Vegas showgirl than a catwalk model. Why do you ask?'

Janetta pushed a tendril of hair away from her face, her gloved hand leaving a muddy smear across her cheek.

'It worries me, sometimes, your slaving away down here to get me and the boys through school.'

'There's no slaving about it,' Felice replied quickly. 'I like my work.'

'I know you do, but you should be married with your own family by now. You're the type.'

'Is that what you think? Well, the minute I meet Mr Wonderful I'll drop you all like so many hot bricks,' Felice promised lightly as she dug out the last of the cabbages. 'The trouble is, Mr Wonderfuls never seem to find their way here.'

Until Tobias had come to Woodlands...

The thought came unwanted, unbidden, and Felice chased it away by reminding herself she'd only *thought* Tobias was wonderful in those first moments of meeting—before he'd had a chance to prove he was the very opposite.

'I suppose you're right,' Janetta agreed. 'It would do you good to get off the island for a while. Are you going to return to university when we're off your hands?'

That had always been Felice's plan, but now she wasn't so sure. Somehow, nothing in the future held much appeal since she'd met Tobias. 'I haven't really thought about it,' she replied, ending the conversation by wheeling the barrow away to the compost heap.

When she returned, Janetta had her hands on her back and was stretching. 'My muscles are screaming for mercy. I must be out of practice with this sort of work.'

'I should have eased you in gently,' Felice apologised contritely. 'Would you rather go back home and get a meal ready? Say for six o'clock? That would be a big help.'

'It would be a bigger help to me,' Janetta replied with a rueful grin. 'What shall I cook?'

'Surprise me.' Felice wasn't going to admit that lately she'd gone off her food, or Janetta would be asking questions it would be extremely difficult to answer.

All in all, Felice had lots to ponder on as Janetta left and she carried on working. The casual hands she'd hired were all hard workers, so the work was well on schedule. Seeing the gardens lose their neglected air and become well-tended, almost loved, was about the only pleasure still left to her.

She always felt dissatisfied, peace and contentment a thing of the past, and she constantly had to check herself to stop her unaccustomed misery from showing. She knew very well what the cause was, but the cure was still one she couldn't contemplate.

No, she told herself grimly, she just had to get on with it until time got her over it. The 'it' being her yearning for Tobias, of course.

Thursday brought a shock in the form of a letter from his solicitors. Pinned to it was the rent cheque. In dry legal terms she was informed that it was being returned because the estate of Joshua Hunter, deceased, had been wound up and closed. Furthermore, his executors took the view that Mr Hunter had regarded her as a caretaker rather than a tenant, so no monies had ever been due.

The letter was signed this time by the senior partner in the firm, and seemed to have nothing whatsoever to do with Tobias. So her determination to prove to him that she wasn't a gold-digger had been a waste of time, and that quite robbed her of her relief at having some financial security again.

Why was it that, whatever she did, Tobias always seemed to triumph?

She was still brooding about it that afternoon when she had to drive into Bixley to tend the garden of a lonely pensioner who wouldn't accept a substitute for her—mostly, Felice suspected, because she always lingered for a cup of tea and a chat, however busy she was.

Afterwards, she stopped off at the cottage before returning to Woodlands. She'd promised to put a casserole Janetta had prepared into the oven. She was just closing the oven door when Janetta burst into the kitchen and accused, 'You sneaky thing!'

'Me? Why?' Felice asked, startled.

'The dogs and I were in the greenhouse at Woodlands when I was grabbed from behind, spun round and jolly nearly kissed. And by the most gorgeous man! At least, I think that was what he meant to do,' Janetta exclaimed, her eyes sparkling with mischief rather than outrage. 'Then I was dropped like a hot coal and told, "Sorry, I thought you were your sister".'

'*Tobias*...' Felice breathed, her heart lurching drunkenly between joy and despair.

'Yes, *Tobias*!' Janetta repeated wickedly. 'Honestly, I could wring your neck. Here's me fretting about you wasting away while you get us through school, and all the time you've got a hunky caveman tucked away. I tell you, I was absolutely gob-smacked!'

'If you picked up that expression at school, you can leave it there,' Felice snapped, her nerves too strung-out to cope with Janetta's amusement. 'I haven't got a hunky caveman.'

'Tell that to Tobias,' Janetta scoffed. 'He's waiting for you right now. Phew! I almost wished I was you.'

'Stay away from Tobias. He's—he's——' Words failed Felice. She couldn't tell Janetta exactly what Tobias was without giving away the whole story. She could only look into her laughing eyes and finish lamely, 'He's best avoided. He seems to think women are toys, there to be played with when it suits him.'

'He seemed serious enough to me. He looked sort of *robbed* when he realised I wasn't you. He must have been fooled by that old leather coat I borrowed from you, and because my hair's in a pigtail, the way you wear yours when you're working. What's more, the dogs didn't go for him, so they couldn't have been as surprised as I was.'

'They like him,' Felice admitted, her mind refusing to work fast enough to fib her way out of this predicament.

'They're not the only ones, are they?' Janetta challenged. 'Oh, come on, now! You surely don't expect me to believe he'd grab you like that if you didn't want him to. If that were true, you'd never go near the place.'

'I told you, I thought he was in Canada,' Felice replied weakly. 'We—I—well, there was a bit of a situation between us but it's finished now. I thought it would be safe to work on the gardens while he was away. You know how I love the place, and the money will be useful.'

'And that's all there is to it?' Janetta questioned, watching her closely. 'I don't mean to be a pain, but Tobias definitely acted as though he had some kind of claim on you.'

'Well, he hasn't.'

'You mean he's fallen for you and you haven't fallen for him?'

'No, I don't mean that.'

'What do you mean, then?' Janetta wasn't laughing now, and, when Felice failed to answer, she mused, 'You haven't been your usual self since I got home. Gosh, don't tell me you've fallen for him and he only fancies you.'

'I haven't fallen for him,' Felice denied vehemently. 'I might have if—if——'

'Yes?' Janetta urged.

'Oh, can't you be a really nice sister and stop asking awkward questions?'

'No!' Janetta wailed. 'I refuse to be treated like some cloistered kid who needs to be protected from real life.'

'Oh, do you?' Felice snapped, her temper fraying as badly as her nerves. 'When it comes to Tobias Hunter, *I'm* the one who needs to be protected. Or I was!'

Janetta's resentment vanished. The sparkle came back into her eyes and she breathed, 'Who'd have thought life on the island could be this exciting?'

Felice's voice almost broke. 'It isn't a joke, Janetta.'

'Heavens, no, it's the most romantic thing I've ever heard. And to think he's waiting for you right now. Doesn't it just make your toes curl?'

'No, it doesn't.'

'It will when I tell you the rest of it,' Janetta predicted.

'What?' Felice asked apprehensively.

'Tobias said that if you don't go to him he'll come looking for you.'

'If he thinks I'm going to go running to him he's got another think coming,' Felice exclaimed indignantly. 'He's obviously too used to people jumping whenever he cares to crack the whip. Me, I'd rather hang about and have some coffee.'

'Good thinking,' Janetta approved. 'Sometimes it pays to be different. What if he comes after you, though? What do you reckon he'll do?'

Felice, setting about making the coffee, shrugged to avoid answering. Not for anything was she going to confess that that particular question was quietly shredding her nerves to ribbons and making the cups rattle. From what she knew of Tobias, he was capable of doing anything.

Janetta was watching her like a hawk, but it wasn't until her sister sat at the kitchen table to drink her coffee that she pleaded again, 'Please, please, tell me what has been going on between you two.'

Felice sighed, 'I suppose I shall have to.' She was too keyed up to sit herself, and so she leaned against a kitchen counter and gave a carefully censored version of the situation between herself and Tobias.

The trouble was that her romantically minded sister was more than capable of filling in the gaps, and colouring with purple passion situations Felice imagined she'd made sound fairly innocuous.

Janetta also managed to wangle further information by asking questions that were very hard to dodge. One that almost floored Felice was, 'What was the last thing he said to you?'

Felice had a searing picture of Tobias in the dusk at Woodlands. She felt scorched again by his arrogant fury, and felt once more the crumpling of her heart as she'd recklessly defied him. She forced some coffee down her reluctant throat and admitted, 'He said he hoped I'd break my damned neck.'

'Wow!' Janetta exclaimed, as though that were the most romantic sentiment expressed since Romeo courted Juliet. 'You really have got under his skin!'

'No, I've got between him and his ego.' Felice was finding it very hard not to watch the kitchen clock. As the minutes ticked by, her bravado was wearing thin. She really didn't want Tobias to come after her. Even less did she want him thinking she was shirking an inevitable confrontation out of cowardice.

'He didn't strike me as an ego-freak,' Janetta replied thoughtfully.

'You don't know the man.'

'I do, sort of. We talked, you know, once we'd sorted out his mistaking me for you.'

'What about?' Felice demanded.

'You, the family, that sort of thing. He was surprised to find out you were a landscape gardener, and even more surprised to learn you were *his* gardener.'

'I can imagine,' Felice said wryly. 'That's why he wants to see me—to give me the sack. Well, there's no point in putting off the evil moment any longer. It's not as though I want to work at Woodlands if he's going to be there.'

'Are you sure about that?' Janetta asked, wrinkling her lovely nose doubtfully.

'Yes, I'm sure. Just promise me you won't mention a word about it to anyone. I'd hate anybody else getting the wrong idea.'

'Mum's the word,' Janetta agreed, although she looked disappointed.

Felice had to be satisfied with that, and as she drove the van to Woodlands with Janetta still chattering beside her she listened with only half an ear. All her thoughts, all her nervous energy, were wrapped up in seeing Tobias again.

In a curious way she felt they'd never really been apart, and that everything that had happened to her without him had simply been a distraction, a diversion from the main stream of her life. Such thoughts didn't do her confidence any good.

She dropped Janetta and the dogs off by the greenhouse where her sister had met Tobias, parked the van and walked through lightly falling rain to the back door of the house. It was open but there was no sign of its new master.

Felice called. Nobody answered. She took off her muddy wellingtons and padded into the huge kitchen in her thick woollen socks. She walked along the service passage until she reached the main one with its ornately carved doors. She stopped again. Tobias was close. She could sense him.

She was so tense it was hard to keep her voice from quivering as she called again, 'Hello? Is anyone home?'

'Hello, Felice.'

Tobias spoke softly. The tiger was purring, then, its claws still sheathed, but as she turned with a painfully pounding heart she warned herself not to be deceived.

'Hello, Tobias.' Her own voice was soft, too soft, but it was the sight of him that weakened her defences. Here, in tall, broad and vibrant life was the phantom of her night and daytime dreams. Her hungry gaze rested on his shock of dark hair, his dark grey eyes and his firm lips . . . those lips that could tease so cruelly or satisfy so blissfully.

He was dressed casually enough in light blue jeans and a round-necked sweater that revealed the strong column of his throat, but his very aura spoke of wealth and power. Suddenly Felice was conscious of what a sorry picture she must look with her windswept plaited hair, and her rough working clothes.

She became acutely conscious of her bootless feet as his gaze roamed slowly over her face and body and came to rest questioningly on her unglamorous woollen socks. She said in a surly voice, 'I left my wellingtons at the back door. They were dirty.'

'The back door . . .' he repeated. 'So that's why I didn't hear you arrive. Why didn't you use the front?'

'The back door seemed more appropriate. It's the tradesman's entrance, after all.'

Deliberately she brought their new relationship into focus. It was a desperate, self-torturing attempt to get this confrontation over and done with.

It might not be what she really wanted, but now that she'd seen him again and all the emotions that had bedevilled her during his absence struck with renewed force she knew they could no longer go on as they were. It would surely be better to make the break between them final and irrevocable.

Wouldn't it?

CHAPTER EIGHT

Now he could fire her, Felice thought, wishing her heart wouldn't pound so painfully. She'd made it easy for him. Any moment the axe would fall. Then she could go away and lick her wounds in private, and hope that some time over the next fifty years or so they would heal.

But Tobias didn't take the opening she offered. Instead, he stood back and held wide the door he'd come out of. It was a silent invitation for her to enter. Felice tried to remember what room it was but she couldn't be sure.

Not a bedroom, anyway, not here on the ground floor, but she was reluctant to be closed in anywhere with Tobias. However large a room might be, there was something about him that seemed to shrink all available space to just the two of them.

And he was being much too quiet, much too restrained. She said uneasily, 'I prefer to talk right here, thank you.'

'Frightened of me, Felice? I thought you were too spirited for that.'

'Of course I'm not frightened of you!' Her denial came from pride, and her pride was always fierce. 'I'm wary of you, and you can hardly blame me for that.'

'I don't, but everything is different now. My female employees never have anything to fear from me.'

'I'm not going to be your employee for long, am I? In fact, you don't have to fire me. I quit.'

'Why?'

Felice was astonished. 'You can't want me working for you!'

'On the contrary, I have a proposition to put to you that will have you working for me in a much closer capacity.' He saw the alarm flash in her eyes and added, 'A business proposition, so stop being foolish and come in.'

Felice was annoyed to find herself obeying, but she was so baffled and intrigued by this new, restrained Tobias that she couldn't do anything else. One way or another, he knew how to keep her guessing.

And hoping, an inner voice sighed...

She ignored it and glanced swiftly round at the book-lined shelves and heavy leather armchairs. She was in the library, a warm library, so the heating had obviously been switched on. She supposed it was as neutral a ground as she could hope for. There was still something very defensive about the way she stood in the middle of the room, though, until she realised Tobias wasn't going to sit down unless she did.

Her strung-out nerves soon told her it wasn't a good idea for her and Tobias to be standing within arm's reach of each other, so she dropped quickly into the nearest armchair.

He reached out and touched her hair. 'You're wet,' he said. 'You should take better care of yourself.'

'Just a little rain. I'll soon dry,' she replied, unable to accept his concern and pulling away from him.

He looked at her for long, thoughtful moments, then shrugged and sat opposite her. His eyes had a brooding quality and almost seemed to devour her. Sitting passively under his scrutiny wasn't easy, far from it, and she couldn't help jumping when he said suddenly, 'I want you to be my housekeeper.'

Felice couldn't have been more surprised if he'd slapped her round the face. 'B-but I'm a landscape gardener,' she stuttered. 'I loathe housework.'

Tobias did something treacherous, then. He leaned across the open space between them and gathered her restless hands in his calm, strong ones. He studied her open palms and murmured, 'Smooth, just as I remember them. You must wear gloves when you're working.'

'Of course I do.' She snatched her hands away, but his touch had already sent sensuous messages tingling throughout her body. It was terrible how the slightest physical contact between them not only awoke her senses but had them sitting up and begging for more.

'You can still supervise the work in the grounds, and I certainly don't expect you to skivvy in the house. In fact, I forbid it,' Tobias told her levelly. 'You can hire all the staff you need to attend to that. The cost isn't important but the objective is.'

'What objective?' Felice asked faintly.

'I want the house fit for a lady to live in, and I want that objective gained in the least possible time.'

'I didn't know you knew any ladies,' she said. She couldn't quite believe her own rudeness, but the penny had dropped with a clang that outraged her. Tobias, the man she might have loved, was asking her—*her*!—to prepare the house she loved for the mistress he intended to install in it.

It was diabolical. The perfect revenge on her for refusing to be his mistress herself! Yet surely even Tobias couldn't be that diabolical! Desperate to believe she'd misunderstood the situation, she asked, 'Why me? Why not an experienced housekeeper?'

'An experienced housekeeper would only see that everything was scrubbed and polished and properly maintained. In other words, Woodlands would be turned from a cheerless mausoleum into an equally cheerless showplace. I want Woodlands to be a *home*, and that's why I need you. You love the place. You could breathe some of that love into it, make it come alive.'

Tobias sounded so sincere, and was so much in tune with her own feelings, that she was actually moved. Then she remembered how skilful he was at manipulating her emotions, and she retorted indignantly, 'You must be mad! I'm not going to work here to be mauled whenever the fancy takes you.'

'Mauled?' he repeated quickly. 'Was that the way it seemed to you?'

Felice bit her lip and looked down at her hands, twisting and turning nervously in her lap.

Tobias followed her gaze and said, 'Relax, Felice. You're completely safe. I've already made it clear I never—maul my employees.'

'You were ready to maul my sister when you thought she was me!'

'I'd no idea you were working for me then, and what happened between Janetta and me was a regrettable mistake which we've sorted out with no hard feelings on either side. By the way, I must congratulate you on the way you've brought her up. She's a fine girl. You should be proud of her.'

Felice looked at him suspiciously, and accused, 'You're trying to side-track me. Whatever you sorted out afterwards, you were still ready to... to...'

'To what?' he prompted when words failed her. When she didn't answer, he went on, 'I was just pleased to see you—what I thought was you. I don't know what's surprising about that. Surely it makes sense, since anything deeper is out of the question, for you and I to be friends?'

'Why?' Felice asked, and she sounded so breathless that she wondered whether, within her, her heart was twisting as nervously as the hands she was trying desperately to still.

'Because I need you.'

Her heart turned over altogether, but mercifully she didn't have to reply because Tobias continued, 'I've been doing some serious thinking about Woodlands while I've been away. The reason I came back earlier than intended was to put my proposition to you. You could have knocked me down with a feather when Janetta told me you were already working in the gardens.'

'That's because I thought the job would be finished before you returned,' she answered, surly.

'I realise that, but, since you're available, taking on the house as well shouldn't cause you any problems.'

'What's causing me the biggest problem right now is that I'm still not convinced it has to be me!'

Tobias stood up. Involuntarily she drew back in her armchair but he walked straight past her. She watched him stop by one of the long windows overlooking the lawn that stretched up to the Grecian temple where last they'd met—and clashed.

She eyed his back and the broad set of his shoulders resentfully. It was soul-destroying, knowing all she did about him and yet still wanting to go over to him, put her arms around him and lean her weary head against his strong shoulders. She could almost feel the contact of her body against his, so powerful was her need, so hard the struggle to resist it.

Fearfully, she finally faced up to the truth that had been causing her so much misery—that if she hadn't fallen helplessly in love with him at first sight then she'd been such a short step away ever since that she couldn't tell the difference.

And she couldn't love him! The man she loved must be prepared to commit himself as fully to her as she did to him, and Tobias couldn't—*wouldn't!*—do that.

'Why you?' Tobias echoed at last. 'The answer is that it could only be you. The proof is out there in the gardens. You've only been working on them for a couple of weeks and already they look—loved. Can you give me the name of another contractor who would give them the same amount of care—as opposed to simply doing a professional job?'

Felice couldn't. That was the trouble with love, she thought resentfully; it showed. She was only surprised that Tobias was sensitive enough to recognise it.

'I thought not,' he said, as the silence between them lengthened. He turned to face her and continued, 'That's why I want you to take on the house as well. I won't be here to supervise much of the time, so I must have complete trust in whoever takes on the job. Feeling the way you do about Woodlands, you're not likely to make any mistakes.'

He wouldn't be here... did that quiver in her heart mean she was glad or sorry? She was so confused that she couldn't tell. She was also beginning to feel pressured, cornered, but in a very subtle way.

Somehow, Tobias was managing to make it sound so reasonable, so right, for her to take on the house—when in her mind she knew nothing could be more unreasonable, or more wrong.

Fighting for time to untangle her emotions, she said, 'Basically the house just needs a thorough spring clean and a few feminine touches, so what mistakes could a professional housekeeper make?'

Tobias returned to the chair opposite hers but this time he sat casually on the arm and leaned towards her. She felt threatened, but deliciously so, as the excitement caused by his closeness pulsed through her body.

She wondered if Tobias knew how she felt, and moving closer was a deliberate ploy to fluster her and affect her judgement. It was more than possible, considering how good he was at playing on her emotions. Look how he was using her love for Woodlands to get her to do what he wanted.

She must resist, be strong, no matter what he said!

But, loving Woodlands as she did, what Tobias said next couldn't fail to get through to her. 'When we first viewed the house together, you said how wonderful it was that some of the rooms are still hung with wallpaper dating back to when the house was built,' he recalled. 'Somebody with an unknowledgeable or unsympathetic eye might decide the paper should be stripped and replaced with something modern.'

'No, that would be vandalism!' Felice cried vehemently. 'That wallpaper is priceless, irreplaceable.'

'Then there are all those oak dressers you admired in the kitchen,' he went on thoughtfully. 'What if they were ripped out to make way for modern equipment?'

'Don't!' Felice's summer-sky eyes darkened with horror. 'There's room enough for improvements without any drastic measures like that. You mustn't let it happen, Tobias.'

'It won't with you in charge, will it?' he pointed out.

Felice felt trapped, and more so as he went on smoothly, 'You will have complete responsibility and, as it's only a temporary position, I'm sure you'll find it more of a challenge than a burden. You don't strike me as a girl to resist a challenge, so shall we consider the matter settled and shake on it?'

He held out his hand. Too late she saw the trap he had steered her into was sprung, and she protested helplessly, 'But I've no intention of working for you!'

'Don't look on it as working for me, look on it as working for Woodlands,' he reassured her.

She would still have resisted, but Tobias smiled at her in that friendly way that had first entranced her, and somehow her hand just found its way into his.

Once more her body was betraying her brain, and once more she inwardly crumbled at his touch. How safe she felt with her hand in his like this, when she was actually about as safe as she would be in a tiger's den. Which, come to think of it, was exactly where she was.

It was her own fault, of course. She'd seen the trap and yet still allowed herself to be beguiled into walking straight into it. For all she knew, Tobias might be getting a perverse kick out of ensnaring her so neatly, and looking forward to her chagrin when she had to hand over the restored house to his mistress.

What an idiot she was to get involved and yet... and yet... when had she really had any choice? Love—no less powerful for being unacknowledged—had dictated all her actions since she'd met Tobias. And love, as she was discovering now, was so much more persuasive than common sense.

She was, as usual, both glad and sorry when he released her hand, and she sounded surly again as she grumbled, 'What I don't understand is why you're suddenly so pernickety about what happens to Woodlands. I thought you hated the place. You were scathing enough when you called it a folly.'

'True, but I didn't know then that a folly could have its delightful aspects.'

Felice looked at him uncertainly. He sounded so ambiguous that for a moment she thought he was referring to her, not to the house. Then she supposed her imagination must be working overtime again. Needing clarification, though, she asked, 'You mean from the point of view of raising children?'

'That as well,' he replied cryptically. 'We mustn't forget the children, must we?'

She was none the wiser but again he smiled, and again her foolish heart lurched. Annoyed with herself, she snapped, 'I don't know who you think you're kidding, but it isn't me. You don't care tuppence about Woodlands. I do, and that's the only reason I'm taking on the job.'

'What do I care about, then, Felice?' he asked softly.

'I don't think you care very much about anything. All you're bothered about is whether the woman you bring here to have your children will take one look at all the neglect and head straight back to the city.'

'No, she won't do that,' he replied confidently. 'When she comes here, everything will be as perfect for her as if she'd organised it herself. It's the very least she deserves.'

Oh, God, he actually had somebody lined up already! There was no mistaking his warmth as he spoke of her. Felice was particularly sensitive to it because she felt so chilled herself. There was even ice crackling her voice as she asked, 'I suppose you expect me to say she's a lucky woman?'

'I never know what to expect from you, Felice, and that's why I'm sure our working relationship will be a very interesting one.'

'You said you wouldn't be here!' she cried.

'I won't be most of the time, but I should manage the odd day or the occasional weekend. There's no reason why that should bother you, is there?'

'No,' she agreed hollowly, since she could hardly do anything else. What was even more soul-destroying was that she knew, from here on in, she would be living for that odd day or occasional weekend...

When Janetta heard the news she exclaimed, 'Golly, Felice! I'm beginning to think you love the man if you've agreed to be his housekeeper! It's not exactly a job that's up your street, is it?'

'It's only a temporary position, and I'm only doing it so that Woodlands isn't spoiled by somebody with no feeling for the place. Besides, Tobias will hardly ever be there,' Felice replied defensively.

'I reckon he's got a nerve expecting you to prepare a nest for his mistress! I'd have told him what he could do with his job!'

Felice just smiled, shook her head, and refused to be drawn on the subject any further. She had so many other things to think about, not least the planning of the best way to set about restoring Woodlands.

After the initial briefing from Tobias, he'd become annoyingly vague. She was to chuck out what she thought was rubbish, install any modern equipment she thought necessary—in fact, do as she pleased so long as she didn't bother him with what he called tiresome trivia.

If she hadn't been so desperately worried about falling deeper in love with him, she would have been in her element, for what he'd actually given her along with a bunch of keys was permission to ransack Woodlands from the attics to the cellars—something she'd been wanting to do all her life.

By the time she was finished, she'd know all the house's secrets...although, of course, she'd still be none the wiser about what went on in the heart of the man who owned all this dusty and neglected spendour.

Perhaps it was just as well that she was too busy to brood too much. Early the next morning she left the dogs with the still-sleeping Janetta and arrived at Woodlands to make a detailed survey of the house to decide exactly what needed to be done, and in what order.

Once she'd sorted that out, she'd know how many staff to hire. She'd noticed yesterday that the heating had been switched on, and she was grateful for it as she left her coat in the kitchen of the home wing and made her way up the magnificent staircase to the second floor.

She'd decided to start on a high—with the bedrooms in the home wing. They'd struck her as needing the least attention when Tobias had whirled her through the house on his initial inspection. Later she would get down to the nitty-gritty of the domestic and the living-rooms.

She went logically from bedroom to bedroom, inspecting wallpaper, paintwork, carpets, curtains, furniture, prints, paintings and ornaments. The scrawlings in the notebook she carried with her lengthened with every room, and she smiled ruefully as it became increasingly obvious that Tobias had no idea of the scale of the job he had thrust upon her.

In his usual autocratic way, he'd said he'd wanted the house put to rights in the least possible time. What, exactly, did he regard as the least possible time? By the time Felice walked into the master bedroom, she'd come to the conclusion that a year would be pushing it!

Her mind was so full of domestic details that she walked up to the huge four-poster with its scarlet hangings and quilts before she realised that the bedclothes were rumpled. She stopped dead and stared in amazement.

This, obviously, had been Old Josh's room, but what was equally obvious was that Tobias was using it now.

She hadn't bargained on that. He hadn't asked her to engage any staff for his own comfort, so she'd assumed he'd only been making one of his lightning day trips. If he'd intended staying overnight on the island, he could have booked into any one of the dozens of comfortable hotels the island abounded with.

Why should a multi-millionaire used to every possible comfort choose to sleep in a house that had been uninhabited for so long? It didn't make sense, but flung across the rumpled bedclothes were a pair of black pyjamas, and who could they belong to if not to Tobias?

Feeling as much of a trespasser as when she used to hide in the grounds, Felice tiptoed across the thick carpet and picked up the pyjama jacket. It was as seductive to her touch as the man himself. Pure silk, with the collar and cuffs ribbed with gold and a flamboyant 'T' embroidered in gold thread on the pocket. She fingered the 'T' lovingly and was fighting off the urge to bury her face in the sensuous silk when a sound made her spin round.

Tobias, naked except for a white towel wrapped casually around his muscular hips, was silently surveying her from an arched doorway. Dear heaven, she'd forgotten the master bedroom had a lavish en suite bathroom! She'd forgotten everything in the need to touch the silken pyjama jacket that now slipped from her nerveless fingers to the floor.

Her wide, defenceless eyes registered that his hair was damp as though he'd just showered, and that his bare chest was glistening with moisture. She was conscious of an ache in the pit of her stomach, an ache that was so severe it was almost a pain.

Tobias looked exactly what he was—a virile, rampant male—and a primitive urge to mate with him parted Felice's soft lips and turned her knees to jelly.

Her hungry eyes roamed over his firm hard body and fixed on the black hair matting his chest. Involuntarily, she followed the dark, tapering line of hair until it disappeared below the fleecy towelling, and she was conscious of the most shameful disappointment that she couldn't see any more.

Too late she realised how blatantly and uninhibitedly her natural instincts were swamping and betraying her, and a slow, fierce blush fired her cheeks and body.

Total panic overcame her as she tried to claw her way back from pure, primitive instincts to conditioned, decently civilised behaviour. The transition was too swift, too contradictory for her to manage with any semblance of composure.

Tobias might be next to naked but she knew the one who was truly exposed here was herself, and she babbled with embarrassment, 'I b-beg your pardon. I wouldn't have b-barged in like this if I'd known y-you were here. I'd n-no idea you'd spent the night here.'

'Felice...' he breathed, as though he hadn't heard a word she'd said. 'My magnificent Felice...'

CHAPTER NINE

FELICE watched helplessly as Tobias's lithe strides cut to nothing the distance between them. How could he have called her magnificent? He was the magnificent one!

Then every thought was blotted out by the primitive call of his bare matted chest and the naked intent she read on his rugged face. *All man*, something deep within her whispered triumphantly. *My man*.

He was right before her, the musky male scent of him filling her nostrils, sensuously overlaying the clean smell of soap on his skin, the spicy tang of his aftershave. Her notebook fell from her nerveless fingers to join his pyjama jacket on the floor.

Then Tobias swore savagely and fluently, and sheered away from her.

'For a moment I forgot you were my housekeeper,' he muttered, picking up a dressing-gown flung carelessly over an armchair. 'Sorry, it won't happen again.'

He shrugged himself into the gown, tied the belt around his waist and turned to face her. 'Sorry about the language, too, but at least I've proved you're safe with me. I hope that means you'll keep the job.'

The job. Yes, of course! Preparing his house to receive his mistress, the one he'd selected to bear his children. How could she possibly have forgotten a thing like that? After all, he no longer really wanted her, Felice Lawson. She'd just happened to be there and, given the right opportunity, a tiger was hardly likely to turn into a pussycat overnight.

'If you'll leave a note downstairs when you're staying over, I won't barge in on you again like this. Now, if you'll excuse me, I'll be getting on,' she replied primly, stooping to pick up her fallen notebook.

As she straightened, Tobias touched her arm. 'There are still some things to be sorted out between us. Give me five minutes and we'll have breakfast together. A working breakfast.'

'Breakfast?' she repeated in dismay, and flinching as his touch seemed to burn through the wool of the long-sleeved blue dress she'd chosen as suitable for her new housekeeping role. 'There isn't a scrap of food in the house. Besides, I've already had breakfast.'

'In that case, we'll go to a hotel, and you can have coffee while I eat.'

'No, we won't!' she exclaimed in alarm. 'If I'm seen breakfasting with you it will be all over the neighbourhood by noon, and nobody's going to believe I'm just your housekeeper then.'

Tobias stared at her with an arrested expression on his face. 'Would that bother you?'

'Of course it would!'

'You're adorable when you're quaint,' he murmured. 'You make me feel I've strayed on to another planet. But I'm still starving, so where can we go that's private enough for us to talk and eat without your neighbours putting two and two together and getting their sums wrong?'

'You'd better come to the cottage,' she replied reluctantly, unable to come to terms with Tobias thinking her either adorable or quaint, and not sure whether it was a compliment, anyway. The adorable bit sounded all right but, given the kind of man Tobias was, the quaint bit could well be the kiss of death.

'I don't want to put you out, but the offer sounds good if you can cope.'

'I can cope,' she assured him. 'The twins haven't arrived home for half-term yet to devastate the larder, so I can guarantee something to sustain you. Er—how long do you need sustaining for?'

'Until I get to London. I'm flying back right after breakfast.'

Felice felt a pang at his leaving again so soon, but it was a pang she'd have to learn to live with. Looking at it coolly, calmly and sensibly, the more he was away, the better chance she'd have of recovering from stupidly imagining herself in love with him.

Unfortunately, it was very difficult to be cool, calm and sensible where Tobias was concerned, and she was far from recovering fifteen minutes later when he was sitting at the big, scrubbed table in the cottage's kitchen, and she was grilling bacon, tomatoes, mushrooms and sausages, and poaching eggs.

No, she was further away from recovery than ever. In fact, she felt almost—complete. Almost ridiculously happy.

She wasn't the least bit flustered by him watching her cook, either. Somehow, with Tobias in a mellow mood and the dogs curled up asleep at his feet, it all seemed so cosy and natural. It was only too easy to forget the antagonism that had caused so much bitterness and misunderstanding between them.

Well, not quite forget, perhaps, but to push it so far back in her mind that she was able to indulge in a little daydream that Tobias wasn't a rich, important man, and she wasn't his unimportant housekeeper, but that they were just man and woman.

Man and wife...

The daydream went too far at that point, and she came
back to reality with a jolt. So good had been the dream,
though, and so evocative the pictures it had conjured
up, that she had to mock it by asking lightly, 'What
heading does this come under in your scheme of things?
Slumming?'

'If this was slumming, everybody would be fighting
for a slice of it,' he answered comfortably. He looked
around the cosy room with its ancient beamed ceiling,
flagstoned floor and well-worn armchairs by the open
fire, and added, 'You have a great capacity for home-
making, Felice. I know you'll do as good a job on
Woodlands.'

That, she thought with a sigh as she heaped food on
to a warmed plate, was as good an illustration as any
that he no longer saw her as a temptress. Well, that
shouldn't upset her, should it? Her biggest grudge against
him was that he'd only ever seen her as a body. She
should be glad, not resentful, that he was becoming
aware she had other possibilities. She couldn't have it
all ways.

And yet . . . and yet . . . she wished that she could.

Why, she wondered, did he have this disturbing capacity for making her so dissatisfied? Every time she
gained an inch with him in one direction, she felt she
lost two in another!

That dissatisfaction, her treacherous inner voice whispered, is love. The unrequited kind. The kind that hurts
the most . . .

'Blue suits you,' Tobias said unexpectedly. 'A frock
suits you. I've never seen you in one before.'

'Thank you,' she replied, flushing slightly, and
covering her confusion by serving his breakfast. 'I don't

get much chance to wear frocks. Jeans are a part of my way of life.'

'Then it's a good thing you're changing your way of life.'

'Only temporarily,' she pointed out quickly.

Tobias neither agreed nor disagreed, but began to eat his breakfast. When he spoke again it was to say, 'This is delicious.'

'I'm all right with the basics but I'm not a dedicated cook,' she confessed, putting toast and a tea-tray on the table, and sitting opposite him. 'A little domesticity goes a long way with me, particularly when it comes to housework. Once I've got a house the way I want it, I'm only too happy to dump the chores on somebody else if I can.'

'That's what you'll be doing at Woodlands.'

'That's one of the reasons I took the job. I don't know why, but I've always preferred to work on the land. I was studying horticulture before I had to give up college. Maybe I should have been born a boy.'

'What a waste that would have been,' Tobias murmured.

There was another little silence between them as Felice wondered how to answer him. Then, to quieten her fluttering pulses, she decided the safest course was not to answer at all. Instead, she poured the tea, and it was only as she was handing his cup to him that she realised she hadn't asked him if he liked tea.

'Drat,' she said. 'Would you prefer coffee?'

'Tea's fine,' he replied easily. 'When in Rome...'

'You drink tea and chew a straw,' she interpreted wryly.

'I prefer to chew toast, thanks all the same,' Tobias said, biting into a slice. 'It's tastier.'

Felice giggled and, to her delight, Tobias smiled at her in the friendly, uncomplicated way that had so enchanted her when they'd first met. Warmth spread through her, bringing with it self-consciousness, and she reminded him a little shyly, 'You said there were still some things to be sorted out between us.'

'We're already sorting them out.'

'Are we?' she asked dubiously.

'Sure we are. What we really needed was to get to know each other better so we can develop a working relationship we can both trust. I reckon we're doing all right, don't you?'

'If you put it that way, yes, I suppose so,' she admitted slowly.

'Good, then I've gained the main objective of this trip.'

Felice frowned a little over that, and reached absently for a piece of toast. She nibbled it as she asked, 'Does everything have to have an objective with you?'

'Doesn't it with you?'

'I don't know. I've never really thought about it, but then I'm not obsessed with business.'

'Neither am I all of the time. I make decisions and then I delegate. That's what my staff is for, to give me time for a private life.'

'Time for Woodlands,' she mused, finishing her toast. 'Time for folly.'

'I wouldn't call it that, not any more. Whatever Woodlands is, I'm serious about it now.'

Yes, Felice thought, you certainly are. There was nothing more serious than planning a background for a relationship permanent enough to have children. She asked quietly, knowing that his answer might hurt, 'Am I right in thinking you've chosen the woman who'll—who'll——?'

'Share my life and bear my children?' Tobias finished for her. 'Yes, I've chosen her.'

His answer did hurt. Too much. It was a moment before she could catch her breath enough to say, 'It seems strange to me that you're not consulting her about the restoration of the Hall.'

'I'll worry about her. You worry about Woodlands,' he replied forcefully enough to discourage further questions. Then he asked one of his own, 'Where's your sister?'

Felice's mind was reluctant to leave the unknown woman willing to accept the terms which she'd found so objectionable, and she answered absently, 'Janetta's sleeping in. She had a date last night with Tom, a local farmer's son.'

'Do you ever take time off?'

'Not a lot,' she admitted. 'Driving a taxi at weekends rather restricts my social life.'

'Driving a taxi is something you won't have to do while you're working for me. In fact, I forbid it.'

'Oh, do you?' she exclaimed, her blue eyes sparkling with indignation. 'On what grounds?'

'On the grounds that I want all your energy devoted to Woodlands; and that you'll be so well paid you won't need to knock yourself out for some extra income.'

Far from being mollified, Felice retorted, 'You can't dictate what I should or shouldn't do for twenty-four hours a day.'

They were glaring at each other, teetering on the brink of another quarrel, then Tobias said unexpectedly, 'You're right. I shouldn't dictate to you. What if I make it a request? It would bother me if I thought you were working yourself into the ground.'

'You don't have to worry about me. I'm as tough as they come,' she replied, unable to accept that Tobias actually sounded worried about her. If she started believing that, next she'd be believing he actually cared about her! And he didn't. All he cared about was getting Woodlands fit for his mistress to live in.

'You don't seem so tough to me,' Tobias said softly, and she was almost beguiled into believing there was a caress in his voice. Clearly a case of wishful thinking!

She still felt jumpy and confused, though, and capitulating seemed to be the quickest way of getting herself back on even keel. 'All right,' she conceded. 'A request, I can live with. I just won't be forced.'

'As I well know,' he murmured, and he smiled at her in a way that made her feel more confused than ever. There was a quality in his smile that made her remember again the good moments they'd shared, before the bad moments had spoilt everything. It was like glimpsing a dream that should have died, but had somehow taken on a life of its own.

Before she had time to get her guard up again, Tobias extended his hand across the table and said, 'We're learning to give and take, Felice, and that's what friendship is all about. Shall we shake on being friends?'

She was so astounded that her hand found its way into his before she'd had time to think about it. His strong, warm clasp reminded her of how vulnerable she was, and she reacted defensively, grumbling, 'I wish I could be sure who's doing the giving and who's doing the taking.'

'We both are,' he replied confidently, 'and there's no reason why we shouldn't both be happy with that. For the moment, anyway.'

For the moment? What did he mean by that? Felice
had no time to find out, because he was rising from the
table and saying, 'Thank you for breakfast. Can I ask
one more favour? I need a lift to the airstrip. I'm having
a couple of cars sent down so I won't have to bother
you again in future. Oh, yes, and a lot of electronic
equipment will be on its way to Woodlands in a few days'
time so that I can keep in touch with my various offices
while I'm down here. Pick out a suitable room for an
office and the men who deliver it will do the rest.'

He was all business now, and Felice had to gather her
scattered wits in a hurry to suggest, 'The library. . . ?'

Tobias thought for a moment, then shook his head.
'No, the library should be a family-room. Apart from
that, I'll leave the choice to you.'

It seemed to Felice as she drove Tobias to the airstrip
that he was leaving an awful lot to her, and that the
woman he eventually brought to Woodlands might be
understandably resentful, to put it mildly. Still, that was
his problem. She, heaven help her, had enough of her
own. . .

Vivid recollections of the good moments she'd shared
with Tobias continued to haunt Felice over the following
days as she threw herself body and soul into bringing
Woodlands back to life. Moments like the warmth of
their clasped hands, the illicit pleasure of her body
pressed against his, the smiles when things were going
well between them, the reconciliations after they couldn't
have gone worse. . .

All in all, as she frequently reminded herself, it was
just as well she was so busy. Under her capable direction, the cleaners and handymen she'd hired were

turning Woodlands upside down and putting it back together as good as new.

Apart from the routine work, she called in specialists to shampoo carpets, clean paintings, check the electrical wiring, the central heating and the plumbing; and agonised herself over the choice of new equipment to harmonise with the character of the kitchens and utility rooms.

It was a big responsibility, but a still bigger delight to spend lavishly without having to spare a thought for the cost. After so many years of careful budgeting at the cottage, it was as if every day was Christmas at the Hall.

Sometimes she even forgot she was buying for another woman's benefit, and would find herself behaving as though Woodlands was indeed her own. Then she'd pull herself up sharply, give herself a good talking to, and try to kid herself that such lapses wouldn't happen again.

They always did, but somehow her lapses were all wrapped up in these frantically busy days being both the saddest and happiest of her life. Beguiled by the atmosphere of the house she loved so much, it was easier— kinder!—to lose touch with reality than anticipate having to hand it over to its new mistress.

At least when that moment came, she'd have the consolation of knowing that nobody could have made a better job of restoring the Hall than she had. Love, as she had learned the hard way and Tobias had so surprisingly noticed, definitely showed.

By the end of her first week as housekeeper, a kind of organised chaos characterised the home wing of Woodlands, but a few rooms had received such concentrated attention that they were ready for immediate occupancy.

Tobias would be a lot more comfortable the next time he made one of his lightning visits. In addition, a Range Rover and a silver Jaguar were waiting for him in the gothic coach house that had served Old Josh as a garage. Felice was waiting for him, too, every minute of every day, but that was something else she didn't care to dwell on too much.

He'd given her his personal phone number when they'd parted at the airstrip, telling her she could reach him wherever he happened to be if she needed him. Well, she *had* needed him many, many times, but she'd never actually contacted him.

She'd always decided sorrowfully that decisions important enough to her to be shared would probably only be regarded as trivia by him, and he'd made it only too plain that he didn't want to be bothered with that.

What she really wanted, she knew, was his approval, but that was another need that didn't bear looking into too closely. Instead, she discussed any knotty problems that arose with Janetta, and roped in her brothers, too, as they were now home.

Garth and Gavin had brought with them all the exuberant gaiety of sixteen-year-olds, plus empty stomachs, piles of dirty washing and endless anecdotes about the matches they'd played on their rugby tour. What they hadn't brought with them was the glow that usually filled Felice when the Lawson family was complete. This time there was still an empty place in her heart.

Tobias's, of course, except that he wasn't family and scarcely even a friend, no matter what he said. Besotted as she was with him, she could still see that his change of attitude towards her had happened only because he'd realised how useful she could be to him.

But that, and all other considerations, fled from her mind when she looked out of the leaded library windows late on Friday afternoon and saw Tobias step from a taxi.

A happiness she couldn't suppress surged through her as she left the bowl of flowers she was arranging on a side-table and stepped closer to the window. As if aware of the intensity of her gaze, Tobias glanced her way and saw her.

He smiled and waved. She smiled and waved back, and she very nearly topped that by rushing out to meet him. Fortunately, caution filtered through the euphoria of seeing him again, reminding her that he'd scarcely expect his housekeeper to throw herself in his arms!

Oh, but it was so *good* to see him again, and nothing that had happened between them in the past or might happen in the future could alter that...

Felice tried to be sedate as she returned to arranging the flowers, yet she couldn't stop her fingers from trembling, nor her eyes from watching Tobias pay off the taxi and walk towards the entrance to the Hall until he was lost from her view.

He was home! Now she felt complete! Deep down she knew her happiness was only an illusion, as it always was where Tobias was concerned, but that didn't stop her heart thumping out its wild song of joy.

Nor did it stop her spine contracting as he entered the library a few moments later. She didn't hear him come in so much as sense him, and she forced herself to remain with her back to the door as though unaware of his presence.

'Felice.'

The quiet, almost joyful way he had of saying her name sometimes nearly destroyed her self-control. She made herself turn slowly to face him, as though her eyes weren't starved of the sight of him, her heart not hungry for his beloved presence.

Beloved? Where had that word come from? Her subconscious, obviously. She would have to have severe words with her subconscious...

'Hello, Tobias,' she said with a lightness that belied the crazy hammering of her heart. 'Welcome back to chaos, but we're almost at the stage where we're beginning to win.'

'From the appearance of this room, it looks as though it was no contest,' he said, gazing around him appreciatively. He came right over to her, took a daffodil from her hand and twirled it absently between his fingers as his eyes held hers.

Felice retrieved the daffodil and thrust it into the sponge at the bottom of the bowl that was holding her flower arrangement in place. 'Don't be deceived by this room,' she replied, with the same determined lightness. 'It's one of a very few that are so far fit to live in. If I'd known you were coming home, though, I'd have lighted the fire to make it extra welcoming.'

'You said home,' he replied slowly.

Felice flushed slightly, and kept her eyes on the last daffodil to be added to the bowl. 'Sometimes I forget you have so many that this one's hardly special.'

'I wouldn't say that,' he replied, more slowly still. 'I've got a lot of places to live, but I've never stayed in any of them long enough to think of them as home. It comes as a bit of a shock to realise I'll soon have a real one at last.'

She caught her breath, then whispered, 'Poor Tobias. You've got so much, and yet most people with next to nothing have a real home to go back to. Nothing as grand as the Hall, of course, but home is always home. Special.'

'Good God, you're sorry for me!' he exclaimed, looking thunderstruck.'

'Well, I won't be for much longer, will I?' she soothed. 'Woodlands will soon be as much of a home as you or anybody else could wish for.'

'Including you?' he questioned sharply.

'Including me,' she replied with a sigh she couldn't quite suppress.

'Then it's not "poor Tobias" but "lucky Tobias", isn't it?' he replied obscurely. Before a puzzled frown had time to draw Felice's eyebrows together, he took her arm and continued with a smile, 'I want to see how the rest of my *home* is coming along. Show me the other rooms you've made habitable.'

His clasp on her arm was light, but Felice was nervously conscious of his strong fingers as she led him out of the library, along the hall and into the sunny parlour she'd chosen as his office. Its long windows overlooked the gardens and, beyond, the meadows and the sea. It was just the room she would have chosen for herself if she'd had to be shut in with computers, telephones and fax machines.

Tobias's eyes roamed over the equipment, lingered on the potted ivy and other plants she'd spent so much time choosing for the maximum softening effect, and then looked at the view outside the windows. 'Do you always try to bring the garden into the house?' he asked.

'Yes,' she replied unequivocally. 'If you don't like it, you need another housekeeper. It's a case of love me, love my flowers.'

'I'll remember that,' he promised.

Felice flushed. 'I didn't mean that the way it sounded! I just meant—meant—oh, you know what I meant!' To get herself out of her flounderings, she pointedly changed the subject. 'Are you happy with your office?'

'Very. What's next?'

He seemed to have forgotten he was still holding her arm, so, rather than make a fuss by pulling away, she decided the best thing she could do was appear to forget as well. 'Your bedroom,' she replied. 'I've concentrated on the rooms you're most likely to use when you're down here.'

'What a good housekeeper I've found for myself,' he murmured, as they went along the passage and up the gracious oak staircase to the next storey.

Felice thought it wisest not to reply, but she couldn't quell a glow of satisfaction as he inspected the rejuvenated master bedroom. Everything in the room had either been dry-cleaned, shampooed or polished, so that it was bright and gleaming, with every sign of neglect banished. The final touch was the living, crimson blaze provided by bowls of freshly picked tulips.

Tobias looked at the flowers and said, 'How could you have expected me, when I didn't know I was coming back myself until a few hours ago?'

'I thought a good housekeeper should anticipate,' she answered primly.

Tobias looked closely at her and asked sympathetically, 'Is it very hard to be a good housekeeper?'

'Sometimes,' she admitted, caught off guard.

'I thought it might be.' He let go of her arm and raised his hand to lightly brush the back of his fingers across her cheek.

Felice would have been less dismayed if he'd seized her in his arms and tried to ravish her, because that would have been the Tobias she knew. But this light touch across her cheeks was tender, almost loving, and that was when he was at his most dangerous—because then he was the Tobias that she wanted.

'I haven't been too kind to you, have I?' he asked softly. 'You must think me the most selfish brute alive.'

She should have agreed with him, but something within her had never quite accepted that view of him, and she heard herself denying, 'No, I wouldn't say that.'

'Then what would you say?' he asked, and his eyes were so searching that Felice had the heart-stopping feeling he was deliberately pushing their relationship one step further.

But one step further than what?

CHAPTER TEN

'I'D SAY that—that—sometimes you rush too fast to-wards —towards whatever objective you—you happen to have in mind,' Felice stuttered, her words not coming easily because she'd never considered this side of Tobias before and she was unsure of her ground. 'That might be a good thing in business, but—but in private life it might seem selfish, when it isn't really.'

'You make me wonder what I've ever done to make you so kind to me,' he answered, with a self-deprecating grimace.

'I'm not kind, I just happen to believe that everybody deserves a fair crack of the whip,' she replied, embar-rassed. She was also uneasy because they seemed to be drawing closer together. Afraid of reading more into it than was actually there, she continued, 'I'll leave you to get settled now. The kitchen's stocked with basics like coffee and tea, so if you want anything just use the intercom.'

She tried to leave before he could reply, but he de-tained her with a light touch on her arm. 'Why don't we go out to dinner tonight?' he suggested. 'My way of saying thanks for all you've achieved at Woodlands so far.'

Felice was caught on the hop. She wanted to go out with him more than anything in the world, but she couldn't forget the mystery woman waiting to come to Woodlands, nor could her pride tolerate his motive for asking her. 'No thanks necessary,' she replied stiffly. 'You're paying me well for what I'm doing, remember?'

He looked at her long and hard, then said, 'All right, let's forget the thanks and dine together anyway. Just for the hell of it.'

'What do you mean, just for the hell of it?' she asked suspiciously.

Tobias hesitated, then answered slowly. 'I could do with some company.'

Any company, Felice thought mutinously, and that just wasn't good enough. No way was she going to be a substitute for his mistress! She lifted her head proudly and lied, 'I'm sorry, I already have a date.'

'Tomorrow night, then?'

What was it with him? Did his own pride make him incapable of accepting a refusal? Yes, that must be it, she decided, and shook her head. 'Sorry, I'm busy then as well.'

His eyes darkened and Felice left the room hurriedly, anxious to avoid a quarrel. She spent what was left of the afternoon keeping well out of his way. He seemed to have got the message, though, because he didn't seek her out.

She couldn't help being a little peeved about that, although it bore out what she'd suspected—that he'd asked her out because she was the only woman he knew on the island.

Still, being under the same roof as Tobias and knowing they might come face-to-face at any moment drained what few emotional reserves she had left. She felt like a wrung-out rag when she returned to the cottage that evening.

The twins, like Janetta, were helping out in the gardens of Woodlands, and the early dusk meant they'd finished work and arrived home before her. Garth and Gavin were upstairs but Janetta was in the kitchen preparing a mixed grill.

She turned an eager face towards Felice and asked, 'Is it right what I heard? That the lord and master is back?'

'Whose lord and master?' Felice scowled, slumping into an armchair by the fire and closing her eyes wearily. It was an emotional weariness she was suffering from, and somehow that seemed worse than the physical kind.

Sighing, she went on, 'If you mean Tobias, yes, he's back, but he's not my lord and master. I just happen to work for him, no more and no less than that.'

'You two have been quarrelling again!' Janetta accused.

'We haven't. We no longer have the kind of relationship that leads to quarrels.'

'You mean you don't fancy him any more?'

'I——' Felice broke off, her heart stopping as she heard a car with a powerful engine turn into the driveway.

'That's not him, is it?' Janetta exclaimed, reading her mind and running to the kitchen window to peer out into the darkness. 'Oh, my God,' she went on in an entirely different tone, 'it's a BMW. That means Serena! What ill wind's blown our darling cousin here?'

Felice, feeling that her powers of endurance had already been tested enough for one day, entirely agreed with her, but she still felt compelled to scold, 'Oh, do hush, Janetta. Serena might be a bit of a trial but she's still family.'

'A bit of a trial?' Janetta echoed sceptically. 'She's a monumental pain in the——'

'Hush!' Felice hissed again, and much more fiercely, as Serena sauntered into the kitchen like visiting royalty.

Her doll-like face was beautifully made-up, not a wisp of her gleaming fair hair was out of place, and not even the rigours of the mainland motorways and the island car ferry had dimmed her stunning beauty.

She was zipped into a white couture jumpsuit and she had a white leather make-up case looped over one arm. Over the other arm she carried a pile of plastic-wrapped outfits. She dumped these burdens on the kitchen table and exclaimed, 'Darlings, how lovely it is to see you again.'

'If we believe that, we'll believe anything,' Janetta retorted frankly.

Serena laughed, and confessed, 'Oh, all right, then, perhaps I have an ulterior motive...'

'A motive called Tobias Hunter? Janetta guessed shrewdly. 'How did you hear about him?'

'When a Press baron lands in your back yard, you can't expect to keep him to yourself, lovey. Not with newspapers being what they are. I read about his little windfall, and thought a long-delayed visit to my dear cousins might be amusing. Er—my sources of information are correct in advising me he's down for the weekend?'

'Yes, but he's not likely to be interested in you. He's much more interested in Felice,' Janetta retorted with a misplaced loyalty that made her sister groan inwardly. 'She's his housekeeper.'

Serena's blue eyes widened and swivelled to Felice. 'So you've finally got fed up with sloshing about in mud and manure, have you, darling? Or are you being rather clever?'

'I'm supervising the restoration of Woodlands, if you call that clever. It's only a temporary position, but it's useful until my gardening work picks up again in the spring,' Felice replied with a lightness she was far from feeling.

'So that's the way it is,' Serena mused. 'Well, the fact that you've got your feet firmly over the doorstep at Woodlands might come in handy. Tobias could be so useful to my career, considering he's got a finger in every sort of media pie. Tell me, what manner of beast is he?'

'Why does he have to be a beast?' Janetta interjected indignantly.

'It's in the nature of man, lovey, especially the rich ones.' Serena turned to Felice again and asked, 'Or is Tobias different? He doesn't run with the rat-pack and guards his privacy so fiercely that I've never met him. What do you make of him?'

'I don't believe in pre-formed opinions,' Felice told her quietly. 'It's much fairer to make your own.'

'Do I detect an atmosphere?' Serena purred. 'Poor darling, hasn't the big man taken any notice of you? That's hardly surprising, considering what a dyed-in-the-tweed country bumpkin you are. Heaven knows I've offered to take you in hand enough times, but you've never prised yourself out of the mud long enough to come up to London.'

'There was never enough time or money,' Felice was goaded into replying.

Serena studied her more closely. 'You know, you're looking and sounding a trifle peaky, darling. Is all this slavery getting to you at last? I warned you the day would come when you'd regret taking on the youngsters. Talk about a thankless task! Kids just don't appreciate martyrs, do they?'

'I don't regret anything, and I'm not a martyr,' Felice snapped, 'so take your claws out of me. I've had a long, hard day and any blood that's drawn is likely to be yours.'

Serena's eyebrows rose. 'My, you are touchy today!' Her eyes rolled expressively towards the ceiling as a thump sounded upstairs and she went on, 'Don't tell me your baby brothers are home, bless their little cotton socks. Now I can understand your nervous state. There's nothing more trying than a family gathering, is there?'

'We were doing all right until you came,' Janetta grumbled.

Felice frowned at her, then told Serena, 'Yes, the twins are home. They're also over six feet tall, with appetites to match, and you could stuff pillows into their little cotton socks. They're sixteen now, you know.'

'Sixteen!' Serena flew over to a wall mirror and studied her reflection. What she saw seemed to reassure her because she relaxed and cooed, 'Well, that's hardly surprising, I suppose. I wasn't much more than a baby when they were born, after all.'

'A baby?' Janetta marvelled. 'I was the baby, and I'm ten years younger than you. Even Felice is younger than you.'

Felice couldn't help smiling, but Serena scowled and gathered up her outfits. Moments later she recaptured her customary sweetness, however, and said, 'I think I'll eat out. I wouldn't want to get in the way of the lions' feeding time, and I really should pay a call at Woodlands. I wouldn't want Tobias to think we're not neighbourly down here. Same old guest room, is it, darlings?'

She drifted out of the room and Janetta said sourly, 'If somebody could package her, she'd sell better than saccharin. Felice, if you want Tobias, fight for him. Once Serena's got her claws into him——'

'Serena is wasting her time,' Felice replied quietly. 'Tobias already has a mistress to install at Woodlands as soon as it's ready.'

'Oh, you poor thing! I know you're still nutty about him. I just know it!'

A strained smile touched Felice's lips momentarily, lighting her face before extinguishing as though the effort had been too much. 'Then keep it to yourself, there's a honey,' she begged. 'Or should I say "lovey"?'

'Don't you dare! I want to beat Serena's head in every time she calls me that!'

'I know, but she won't stay long,' Felice comforted her. 'Tobias has a very forceful way of dealing with women on the make.'

But Serena dined out with Tobias that evening, and Saturday as well. Felice, feeling she had to back up her lies to him about having dates, went out with Charles. Since all Charles wanted to do was talk about Tobias and hope he'd have further business commissions from him, though, neither evening was very successful.

The days were hazardous enough, as well, since Serena couldn't resist gloating about her conquest of Tobias, and Janetta's eyes were full of unspoken sympathy whenever they dwelt on her suffering sister.

When Serena left for London on Sunday afternoon because she had a modelling assignment the next day, she said to Felice and Janetta, 'I'm working on Friday so I won't be back until Saturday, darlings. It's the country club's annual charity bunfight, isn't it? I've dropped a word in Tobias's ear about it so I expect he'll escort me. Anything special you'd like me to bring down when I come?'

'Just your own sweet self,' Janetta mocked. Then she horrified Felice by adding with youthful and devastating frankness, 'Are you sleeping with Tobias?'

'Don't be silly, lovey,' Serena replied, amused. 'I want something from the man, and I'd be silly to sleep with him before I get it.'

Felice went quite cold. That was the syndrome Tobias recognised and hated—and yet he was tolerating it from Serena. Why? Because he'd fallen victim to her incredible beauty? She felt a pain that was unlike any other pain she'd ever experienced. It wasn't jealousy. It was even worse. It was despair.

She just wanted Serena to go, and could have screamed when Janetta delayed the moment by persisting, 'What exactly do you want from Tobias? To marry him?'

'What a tempting thought, but I don't believe in beating my head against a rock.' Serena replied laughingly. 'Tobias isn't the marrying kind. I'm not sure I am, either. Not yet, anyway. No, I want to get into TV commercials, and he can fix it for me.'

Felice said hesitantly, 'Can't you fix it for yourself?'

'I've had auditions, darling, but I've been told I'm too beautiful for the average woman in the street to identify with, and identifying is all the rage at the moment. Tobias, though, is powerful enough to kick that little stumbling-block aside.'

She smiled and went out to her car, leaving a trail of perfume behind her. Both sisters waited until they heard her car start up and drive away, then Janetta burst out, 'You could give her a run for her money if you wanted to, Felice. You're every bit as lovely as she is.'

'Don't you mean there's so much more of me than there is of her?' Felice mocked wryly.

'So you're not as thin as a rake and you're too tall for most men. So what? You're a real woman and your height doesn't matter with Tobias because he's tall himself.'

'What matters,' Felice pointed out sadly, 'is what Serena just said. The man's only interested in mistresses and I'm only interested in being a wife. And I won't share him, either, which is what it would boil down to, considering the way he is.'

'You could make him love you!'

'No, I couldn't. Love is either freely given, or it isn't given at all. You'll realise that when you're older.' She turned away as the twins came boisterously into the sitting-room, the dogs leaping about them, and there wasn't a trace of sadness in her voice as she asked, 'Where are you two off to?'

'Walking the dogs,' Gavin replied. 'Care to come?'

'No, thanks. I'm going to give Janetta a break from the kitchen and cook the dinner myself. I suppose I can depend on you to get back by six? It will be pitch black then.'

'Sure thing,' Janetta replied for the boys. 'I feel like a walk so I'll go with them. You won't catch me being late when there's a roast in the offing.'

Felice, left to her cooking and her thoughts, spent a thoroughly miserable afternoon. The swift way Serena had been able to ingratiate herself with Tobias showed just how transitory and unreliable his emotions were. Not her sort of man at all! But, oh, she did love him so!

There was no use pretending any longer that she didn't, and she despaired of ever finding anything that would break the steadfast grip Tobias had on her heart. Disillusion alone couldn't do it, or she'd have been cured weeks ago.

The meal was just about ready to serve up, and she was making the gravy when she heard a car stop in the driveway. For a moment she thought it was Charles calling on the off chance that she'd go out with him again, but then there was a commotion of laughter and barking and the door burst open.

In tumbled the dogs, the twins, Janetta—and Tobias. Felice froze. Then, only one logical reason for his visit occurring to her, she said to him, 'Serena's left, I'm afraid.'

'Oh, he knows that!' Garth told her carelessly. 'Felice, the most marvellous thing! We found this old kite in one of the attics at the Hall and Tobias let us fly it. It was cracking fun.'

'Yes, and there are some super fishing rods, too, and he's said we can try them out!' Gavin exclaimed. 'You can't imagine the stuff that's stored away up there!'

'What I can't imagine is what you were doing in the attics in the first place,' Felice replied. She switched her attention back to Tobias and added awkwardly, 'I hope they haven't been making nuisances of themselves.'

'No, we haven't,' Janetta chipped in indignantly. 'We weren't even trespassing. We just happened to be walking the dogs when we met Tobias and he invited us in.'

'Yes, and he flew the kite as well,' Gavin elaborated. 'What's more, he's coming fishing with us next weekend, which is our last one before we go back to school. He's letting us fish the river at Woodlands, too, which we've never done before! We thought the least we could do was invite him home for dinner. It's bound to be better than a hotel meal.'

Felice, unable to picture Tobias flying a kite with her boisterous family, far less going fishing with them, looked helplessly at Tobias. He said quietly, 'If it's convenient ... ?'

'Of course it's convenient,' Janetta affirmed, taking the greatest care to avoid Felice's accusing eyes. 'My sister doesn't cook often, but when she does there's enough for an army.'

Tobias was still looking questioningly at Felice, and she heard herself saying politely, 'Naturally you're welcome, although it's just a family sort of meal.'

'Sounds like the best kind,' Tobias replied, smiling in the way that always made her go weak at the knees. 'Do you need any help?'

'I'll help as soon as I've washed and changed. You lot get out of the way,' Janetta replied, driving Tobias and the twins before her from the kitchen as unceremoniously as if he were just another brother.

Felice found herself alone, staring bemusedly at the gravy. She was still staring at it when it boiled up and over the edges of the saucepan. That brought her out of her trance. She removed the pan from the heat and went over to the wall mirror to stare at herself.

Her face was flushed from cooking, her hair was caught up in a pony-tail, and there was a starry look in her eyes that frightened her. Fiercely she reminded herself of his mistress, of Serena, and of goodness knew how many other women he was probably stringing along.

That took the stars out of her eyes but she still felt she was living at a higher, more vital level—the way she always did when Tobias was close.

The beef was on the carving platter and she was just about to transfer the vegetables to heated dishes when Janetta came back, having hurriedly washed and changed into a pink wool frock. She lifted a pinafore from a hook behind the kitchen door, and said as she threw it on, 'I'll finish that. You whizz off and change. Let your hair down, too. Now's your chance to outshine Serena!'

'You must be mad! I couldn't outshine Serena in a million years.'

'You can do it in seconds. She's only a clothes horse. Just remember what I told you earlier—you're a real woman.'

Felice stared at her in horror. 'You plotted all this! Oh, how could you? I could die of embarrassment! Don't you realise this must be the last place Tobias wants to be? You must have invited him here in a way that he couldn't refuse. I know you did!'

'No such thing,' Janetta retorted blithely, pushing her towards the door. 'I just mentioned we had to be going because you were cooking a roast, he said that sounded great, so I said come and join us, and he did. What's the big deal?'

'You're meddling, that's the big deal. You're doing me no favours, Janetta, honestly you're not.'

'Phooey! It's Tobias who's getting the favours. He might be a multi-millionaire but he's *starved* of all the things we take for granted—family, fun, home-cooking...'

'Since when have you become an expert on Tobias Hunter?' Felice exclaimed.

'Since you started making such a botch of it. Look, I just want Tobias to see you as you really are, then I'll never meddle again,' Janetta promised.

'Can't you get it through your thick head that I've no intention of joining his harem? I could have done that weeks ago if I'd wanted, and without any help from you.'

Gavin came into the kitchen, asking, 'What's the hold-up? I'm starving.'

'So are we all,' Janetta told him, greeting his appearance with relief. 'Don't worry, I'm serving up now and we'll eat as soon as Felice gets changed.'

Felice had no choice then but to run upstairs and search for a frock that was dressy without being too dressy. She hurriedly settled on a frock of fine cream wool, draped from the shoulders to the hips where it was loosely belted before it fell in fluid pleats to just below her calves.

It made her look incredibly elegant, but it also made her feel incredibly tall, and she was frowning at herself as she brushed her hair. She let it fall loosely to her shoulders, added a quick touch of pink to her lips and blue to her eyelids, and hurried downstairs.

When she went into the sitting-room Tobias stood up, and she didn't feel so incredibly tall, after all, but just about right. 'You look like a Greek goddess,' he said, and he sounded so sincere that Felice caught her breath.

Garth glanced at them and asked innocently, 'Aren't Greek goddesses dead, and armless with it?'

Felice chuckled, Tobias laughed, and suddenly everything was all right. They just seemed a family again, with no awkward guest, not that anybody had ever felt awkward about Tobias except herself. But she was over that now, and when they went into the dining-room and began to eat she felt as relaxed and happy as when she'd first met him.

It didn't seem the time to think about conflict and antagonism, and so she didn't. Instead, she indulged in one of her daydreams of how wonderful it would be if they could always be like this, and the dream lasted until long after the meal was over and they sat chatting in the sitting-room. Reality didn't creep back until Tobias stood up reluctantly to leave, explaining that he had to return to the mainland that night.

'Felice will see you to the door,' Janetta said, and instantly Felice was embarrassed again, and no dream, however delightful, was proof against embarrassment. As his hostess, politeness dictated that she see him to the door. How could Janetta have been so crassly obvious, especially after promising not to meddle any more? And why were the boys grinning like that?

Much as she loved her sister and brothers, she could have boxed their ears, and she hoped Tobias wasn't as embarrassed as she was as she also rose to her feet. It was difficult to walk with her usual grace as he followed her out, so conscious was she of him behind her.

In the confines of the passage, she felt even worse. Tobias was so close that the full force of his magnetism hit her, and she had to stiffen every muscle not to sway helplessly towards him. Hating her weakness, she hurried on to the front door.

Tobias didn't seem in any hurry himself, and when he caught up with her, he said with leisurely politeness, 'Thank you for a lovely meal and a delightful evening.'

'You're welcome any time,' she responded, studiously polite herself as she reached nervously for the door handle.

Tobias's lips twisted wryly. 'Give me an open invitation like that and I might make a pest of myself. That's something I'm very good at, isn't it?'

Felice swallowed hard. 'I wouldn't say that.'

'Then maybe I'm making progress,' he replied obscurely. 'Felice . . .'

There was a special deepness, a special softness, in his voice that flustered her. She jerked the door open and shivered violently as a blast of icy air cut through the fine wool of her frock. Tobias's attitude changed, and he frowned. 'Don't stand here catching cold. I'll see you next weekend.'

'There'll be more improvements at Woodlands by then,' she promised, striving hard for normality.

'To hell with Woodlands,' he growled, and went out into the night.

CHAPTER ELEVEN

OVER the next few days Felice was grateful that the restoration of the Hall and its gardens took all her time and energy because, whether she was waking or sleeping, Tobias was always with her. No matter how much of a womaniser he had proved himself to be, or how much she cursed herself for being such a weak and lovelorn fool, he'd become an integral part of her.

Her motivation for living, in fact. That was something she had to come to terms with . . . as soon as she figured out how.

Busy as the days were, though, gossip filtered through to her. The neighbourhood was buzzing with tales of a romance between Tobias and Serena because they'd been seen out together for two nights in a row.

Hearing his name constantly coupled with her cousin's depressed her unbearably. It also reinforced her conviction that, although Tobias complained about women always wanting something from him, he wasn't slow to capitalise when those women happened to take his fancy.

As she once had.

Yet in spite of all this, she couldn't stop herself living for Friday when he would return.

So hungry was she for just the sight of him that when Friday finally dawned, she was at the Hall even earlier than usual, plundering daffodils from the garden to make fresh flower arrangements for the library, and lighting the log fire in the ancient fireplace.

Then she turned her attention to his bedroom, carrying up more vases of flowers, switching up the central heating and checking that her orders for clean bed linen and towels had been properly carried out.

By nine o'clock that morning everything was ready for him, and by half-past four that afternoon he still hadn't arrived. Soon the daily workers would be leaving and unless she waited on he would be returning to an empty house. She didn't want him to do that, even if it would be his own fault for not telling her exactly what his plans were.

As the best part of another hour dragged by, Felice began to wonder if Tobias had decided not to return until Saturday, because Serena wouldn't be back on the island until then.

So much for all the welcoming touches she'd arranged for him! Well, there was no reason for her to be piqued. Tobias wasn't exactly answerable to his housekeeper for his actions, was he? And there was absolutely no reason why she should think she meant more to him than that, just because he meant so much more to her than an employer!

Her staff was checking out in ones and twos when Tobias finally came striding into the Hall, delighting her eyes and senses—and making nonsense of her secret hope that when she saw him again she would be 'cured'.

Just one glimpse of his burly form, his rugged face and dawning smile, and her heartbeat accelerated so much that she knew she was as far from being 'cured' as she had ever been. 'You're late,' she said accusingly, before she could stop herself.

'Have I been missed?' he asked, looking at her intently.

Felice turned away to hide a self-conscious blush. 'I just meant that you're usually home before now.'

'All I like about that is the word "home",' he replied, his grey eyes more intent than ever. 'Haven't I been missed even a little bit?'

Felice thought he was being deliberately provocative. 'You're not exactly living here, so it would be difficult for you to be missed,' she told him repressively. 'We all normally leave around now and I thought you might find returning to an empty house a bit depressing, that's all.'

'You're right, and I'm glad you took pity on me and stayed. What would I do without you, Felice?'

His voice had taken on a caressing note and she looked at him indignantly. Damn the man, he just couldn't stop flirting, even though he knew she wasn't interested in that sort of thing. She'd made it plain enough for long enough!

Her indignation was reflected in her voice as she replied, 'I didn't take pity on you. I was just trying to do my job.'

'And you're doing it magnificently,' he soothed her, then had all her senses running riot again by taking her arm and propelling her into the library. It wasn't fair what his touch could do to her, she thought mutinously. It just wasn't fair!

Nor was it fair the way Tobias kept hold of her arm when they were in the library. He looked around and said appreciatively, 'This room is getting cosier and cosier. How is the rest of the house coming along?'

Felice didn't want to make an undignified fuss by shrugging herself free of his grip, so she said with a primness she was far from feeling, 'All the bedrooms and sitting-rooms in this wing are ready for use, so there's nothing to stop you bringing guests with you if you want.'

'I don't want,' he replied bluntly. 'Not immediately, anyway.'

'Don't you think your mistress might be interested in what is being done here? I know I would if——' She broke off as she realised where her impetuosity had led her.

'If you were my mistress?' Tobias finished for her. 'But you've no intention of being my mistress, have you? Or the mother of my children?'

'No, I haven't,' she retorted, beginning to think he was deliberately playing with her, and haunted once more by the notion that he'd made her housekeeper at Woodlands just to punish her. Oh, how could he? Didn't he realise that loving him the way she did was punishment enough?

No, of course he didn't, because he didn't know she loved him, and he must never find out. She managed to free herself from his grip on her arm by walking over to the fireplace, where she bent down to add another log to the fire. 'Anyway,' she continued, 'the point I wanted to make is that if you do want to entertain guests for the weekend, I can always hire a cook and some domestic workers to make you comfortable.'

'I won't want that sort of staff until I move in properly,' Tobias replied decisively.

'What about your own comfort, then?' she persisted, wishing she could stop worrying about him—even if she couldn't stop loving him. The trouble was, the two seemed inextricably bound together.

'For the moment I can fend for myself.'

'But you can't be used to that!' she objected violently.

'I'm not, so it has a certain novelty appeal. A kind of entertainment value. Do you remember when I said you had entertainment value, Felice?'

Of course she remembered! It was on the very first day they'd met, and the only reason he could have for reminding her of it was to provoke her. So she'd been right, then, in thinking he was getting a kick out of playing havoc with her emotions.

What was more, he'd moved so close that he was standing right over her and instinctively she knew he was waiting for her to raise her eyes to meet his. It was the last thing she wanted to do, and so she kept her head bent towards the fire, hoping he'd think she was more interested in watching the flames lick hungrily around the newly added log than in looking at him.

As she watched, two woodlice that had been nesting in the log ran along the top of it, close to the licking flames. Swiftly she scooped them into her hand. Then she rose to her feet and, carefully side-stepping Tobias, went over to open a window and throw them out into the garden.

As she closed the window again, Tobias said disbelievingly. 'You'd risk burning yourself to save a couple of insects most people would regard as pests?'

'Everything has its place in the scheme of things,' she replied, surprised he should see anything remarkable in her action. 'Why shouldn't I save them? They haven't done me any harm.'

He stared at her. Then he said, his voice deepening so that his Canadian drawl seemed to throb on the air. 'Have I done you any harm, Felice? I think I have, and I can't tell you how sorry I am.'

She felt her heart constrict because he sounded so sincere, then all her defensive mechanisms came into play. She couldn't soften towards Tobias for fear he'd take merciless advantage and start talking about horrible things like terms all over again.

'Do you believe I'm sorry?' he insisted, the same soul-destroying throb in his voice.

Felice forced herself to shrug and reply lightly, 'Oh, I don't bother about anything that's over and done with. I'm strictly a today and tomorrow person. I imagine that answers your last question, too, the one about me remembering you once said I had entertainment value.'

Tobias was quiet for a moment, then he asked, 'Would it help if I said that you still do?'

Again Felice's heart constricted, and again she didn't dare let herself believe what her senses were telling her. How could she, when he had Serena on a string and an unknown mistress lurking somewhere?

All the same, it hurt her a lot more than it hurt him to scoff, 'If you're interested in entertainment value, I'd say it was time to bring on the dancing girls, and that lets me out. It's time I was going home, anyway. I'm late as it is.'

Tobias's voice and attitude changed, and he sounded quite cold as he said. 'By that I gather you're busy again this evening?'

'Very.'

'So busy that you couldn't get un-busy if I asked you to dine with me?'

This time Felice's heart not only constricted, it lurched. Oh, how wonderful it would be to stop fighting him and succumb to what he wanted—what she wanted, even if it wasn't *all* she wanted. She hesitated, momentarily allowing delicious tendrils of temptation to wrap themselves around her pride and silence its objections.

Tobias sensed her weakness and put a strong hand under her chin, forcing her face up to his. 'I think you want to dine with me,' he said. 'I think you just don't know how to admit it.'

Oh, if only he'd allowed her to come to that conclusion herself, instead of driving her too hard and too fast, so that all her pride came surging back to defend her against what she could only see as his arrogance!

'I'm afraid I want to dine with somebody else more,' she blurted out, and was rewarded by him releasing her chin as though he'd been stung—if that could be counted as a reward, she thought miserably.

Tobias turned away from her. 'Then I won't detain you any longer,' he said icily. 'Goodnight, Felice.'

'Goodnight,' she replied, struggling to keep her utter wretchedness to herself.

She succeeded, but wretched was how she remained for the rest of the evening. It was a wretchedness that increased when Serena came swanning in burdened with more outfits than she could possibly wear for one weekend.

'Greetings, darlings,' she cried gaily, bursting into the sitting-room just as the Lawsons were settling down to watch television after dinner. 'My assignment went so well I was able to get away sooner than I expected. Oh, don't move any of you, I'm off again as soon as I've changed. I phoned Tobias while I was waiting for the car ferry at Portsmouth, and he's taking me out to dinner. Must rush, as it seems the beast is starving, and far be from me to keep a starving beast waiting.'

She hurried upstairs, leaving a trail of laughter and perfume behind her. Janetta glowered after her and grumbled, 'I wish she wouldn't call Tobias a beast. Not even you call him that, Felice, and you've got reason if anybody——'

'Oh, hush,' Felice pleaded. 'Serena talks for effect. She doesn't mean half of what she says.'

'Just as well,' Gavin chipped in. 'Tobias is a good bloke. Far too good for her.'

'You can say that again,' Garth agreed. 'Felice, why don't you——?'

'Why don't we change the subject and watch some television?' Felice interrupted desperately. 'I know you all mean well, but please let me lead my own life. I've done my best to let you lead yours.'

That was so true that her sister and brothers were silenced, although Felice was so conscious of their fierce loyalty and furious sympathy that she was driven to bed far earlier than she normally went.

It was a mistake. She lay there tossing and turning hour after endless hour, trying hard not to think of Serena pouring all that saccharine sweetness over Tobias, and being beautiful enough to get away with it.

The fact that Tobias had asked her out first didn't help one bit. It only emphasised what an opportunist he was, she thought wearily, trying to forget how breathtakingly lovely and femininely frail Serena had looked in a pink chiffon gown that was really far too dressy for a dinner date, except that she had the confidence to carry it off.

Felice wondered if she could depend on Tobias being astute enough to realise that Serena was about as frail as the Rock of Gibraltar. Not that it was really any of her business, yet she snapped upright in bed ages later when she heard the front door close and a murmur of voices. One was so deep that it had to be Tobias's.

She looked at the luminous hands of the alarm clock beside her bed and saw that it was just after midnight. She'd heard the twins and Janetta go to bed some half an hour ago, so Serena and Tobias were all alone down there, alone to get to know each other better, and in her home, too!

Felice groaned and pulled the duvet up over her head. She stayed that way until she heard the front door open and close again, to be followed shortly by the sound of a car starting up. She lowered the duvet and looked at the clock again.

Tobias had only stayed fifteen minutes. Was there any hope for her in that, or was Serena still playing an extremely cagey game? Probably, Felice decided with the wretchedness that still had her in its grip.

Not loving Tobias, Serena would be able to manage him much better than she herself could. Love played such games with her senses that her normal judgement and common sense never got a look in. The best she seemed to manage was to stumble erratically from one mistake to another.

Felice groaned again, and once more tried to sleep. Eventually she succeeded but her rest was patchy, long periods of wakefulness interspersed with periods of oblivion that would have been bliss if only they hadn't been so brief.

Eventually she decided that trying to sleep was more exhausting than not sleeping at all. She got up as soon as it was light and moved like a ghost through the still-quiet cottage. The last thing she wanted was to awaken any member of her family. She just didn't feel strong enough to face anybody yet, particularly Serena.

Shortly before eight, muffled up against the bitter cold but still shivering as she went outside, she piled the dogs into the van and drove cautiously down the frost-covered driveway. Ever since she'd started work at Woodlands, she'd used her Saturdays to honour her gardening contracts with those of her customers who didn't want anybody else working for them. She was on her way to one of them now.

As she nosed the van out on to the road, telling herself
that a hard bout of physical work might just make her
feel better, she had to slam on the brakes as a Range
Rover roared by heading for Bixley. The driver's head
turned and grey eyes bored fleetingly into hers.

Tobias!

Felice wanted to go to Bixley, too, and there was absolutely no reason why she should panic, yet instinctively she slewed round the steering-wheel and accelerated
in the other direction.

She was furious with her impetuous, schoolgirlish reaction, but there was nothing she could do about it now.
As if that wasn't bad enough, just that brief glimpse of
Tobias had started the adrenalin pumping through her
veins, bringing her to pulsing, vital life again.

It was only when her pulse-rate began to slow down
that she asked herself exactly what she was so excited
about—the prospect of more emotional punishment?

She frowned and tried to concentrate on the frosty,
slippery road. It was all right for Tobias to zoom along
like that, he had a four-wheel drive. She hadn't, and she
also needed to turn back towards Bixley or face a detour
of several miles.

The driveway to Woodlands was the first opportunity
the narrow road offered, and once she'd circled she drove
slowly, not that there was any chance of catching up
with Tobias the way he'd been shifting. She'd just passed
her home when she was dumbfounded to see Tobias
coming back the other way. He shot past her, slammed
on the brakes and used the cottage driveway to turn again
so that he was behind her.

She couldn't imagine what he wanted with her but she
wasn't hanging around to find out. It was Serena he
should be chasing now, not herself. Her foot came down

hard on the accelerator and she slithered into a bend, managed to straighten and skidded into the next.

She and the dogs sitting up beside her were riding the swaying old van like a bucking bronco while the gardening equipment in the back rattled and crashed about.

It was a mad bid to escape, but it seemed doomed to failure as Tobias closed up behind her. Felice had one thing in her favour, though. She knew every curve, pothole and bump in the tortuous old road, and that knowledge enabled her to stay ahead of him—just.

She also knew all the by-ways and back roads when they roared into Bixley, so that Tobias overshot when she turned off the main road. She soon heard him behind her again but kept turning through the network of lanes until she'd shaken him off long enough to zoom into the driveway she wanted, around to the side of the house and stop out of sight of the road. She switched off the engine and waited. She wasn't cold any longer, she was sweating.

She heard the Range Rover go by, return and then go by again. Tobias knew roughly what area she was in, then. He was searching for her, but he could scarcely trespass into the driveways of all the big old houses along this road. At least, she hoped he wouldn't.

For a few minutes she heard nothing but the frantic beating of her heart, then slowly she relaxed. She'd shaken him off. She still couldn't explain to herself what had made her flee from him any more than she could puzzle out why he'd pursued her so doggedly.

What could he possibly want with her that was so urgent he was prepared to turn the quiet roads of Bixley into some kind of grand prix circuit?

That question was to plague Felice so persistently that she got through her work without ever being aware of doing it. It was still on her mind hours later when she parked the van in the high street to get some fresh bread, newspapers and other odds and ends of shopping. The larder needed constant re-stocking when her brothers were home.

But *what* had Tobias wanted with her?

She was staring in the bakery window, seeing nothing while she tried to fathom out the unfathomable, when an arm came around her waist and squeezed her. She almost jumped out of her skin, then gasped, 'Charles! You nearly frightened me to death!'

'I can't think why,' Charles replied, a little peeved. 'I'm not exactly Dracula.'

No, but you're not exactly Tobias, either, she thought wistfully. For a moment there she'd thought—— Oh, hell! She was going off her head, she really was. As if Tobias would try to cuddle her in the high street!

'What do you want?' she asked Charles, not meaning to sound quite as ungracious as she did.

'The first dance this evening, the last, and all the dances in between,' Charles replied promptly.

Felice looked at him blankly, then remembered that it was the country club's annual charity ball that night. Tobias had driven all thought of it from her mind. She thought about it now and decided that, although Charles was all right, she didn't fancy being monopolised by him all evening. 'Leave yourself some time for propping up the bar,' she countered lightly. 'You men always seem to find dancing thirsty work.'

'Promise me the last dance, then, and a few in between, and I'll offer a fabulous sum for you at auction.'

'That reckless offer could very well cost you a fiver,' she joked, trying to loosen up, be more like her old self. Each year girls were 'auctioned' for the supper dance and the proceeds went to charity. Whoever 'bought' them had the right to the dance and to take them in to supper afterwards.

'Cheap at twice the price,' Charles murmured, giving her waist another squeeze.

Felice was just about to extricate herself from his grip when for some reason her head turned. Standing across the road staring angrily at her from under lowered brows was Tobias. She felt her colour rising as though she'd been caught out in some infamous act, which was ridiculous, because Tobias had no claim on her.

Now, she thought in a flurry of panic, she was about to find out why he'd pursued her so doggedly earlier, but Tobias just swung on his heel and walked away. She was relieved and disappointed, and as if those two emotions weren't conflicting enough she was also more baffled than ever. What had been so urgent earlier that morning that wasn't even worth crossing the street for now?

It was something else to puzzle over while she managed to get rid of Charles, finish her shopping and drive back home.

Janetta was sitting at the kitchen table reading a book. She was wrapped in a bathrobe, her hair a network of huge pink rollers, and only her eyes moved as a mud pack dried to a deathly pallor on her face. 'I'm going to knock Tom dead tonight,' she breathed, trying to speak without moving her facial muscles.

'What's special about Tom?' Felice asked, unaware her sister had any particular interest in the local farmer's son, pleasant though he was.

Janetta stifled a giggle for fear of cracking her face pack, and confessed, 'He's my best bet for bidding a high price for me at the auction.'

'He'd pay double not to dance with you if he could see you now.'

Janetta laughed and her face pack splintered into a thousand pieces. 'Now look what you've made me do,' she wailed.

'With your complexion, you don't need it,' Felice replied, cramming two fresh loaves into one inadequate breadbin.

'Perhaps not, but it's fun to make a special effort. I'm going to borrow Serena's pink chiffon. She'll never wear the same gown twice in a row, will she?'

Felice shook her head. 'I suppose she's still in bed?'

'Where else? She loves her beauty sleep and she didn't get in until midnight.' Janetta paused then continued hesitantly, 'Tobias came in with her. I heard his voice, but he didn't stop long.'

'I know.'

'Felice, I wish you'd——' Janetta began passionately, then broke off and cocked her head as sounds of movement came from the bedroom above. When she spoke again it was in an entirely different tone. 'It sounds as though her ladyship is about to join us.'

'I wish you wouldn't speak about Serena like that.'

'It doesn't bother her. In fact, I think she takes it as her due. Vanity has its own armour, you know, so she must have a hide like a rhinoceros.'

'Well, I always say, if you've got it, use it,' Serena said in amusement as she drifted into the kitchen tying the sash of a black silk dressing-gown around her willowy waist. 'Is that tea you're making, Felice? No sugar for me, darling, and thank you for sending out the boys. I do like to wake up gently on a Saturday morning.'

'I haven't sent them anywhere. I've just got back from work.'

'They're over at Woodlands,' Janetta butted in. 'Tobias said they could use his river to try out some fishing rods they found in an attic.'

'I suppose Tobias is being kind to them because they're my cousins,' Serena smiled, settling herself at the kitchen table in a flutter of silk, and repulsing the cat that tried to jump on to her lap. 'And he's being kind to me, too. I told him having noisy teenagers around the place isn't exactly restful.'

'It's not exactly restful having you here, either,' Janetta retorted. 'Is Tobias taking you to the dance tonight?'

Serena inspected her perfect fingernails for possible flaws before replying, 'No, he has some kind of business to attend to this evening.'

'On a Saturday night?' Janetta asked disbelievingly.

'Men don't get to be multi-millionaires by working regular hours,' Serena replied patronisingly. 'He said he'll look in later if he can. Which means he will.'

'Then you certainly won't be wearing the pink chiffon because he's already seen it. Can I borrow it?'

'If you don't mind Tobias knowing it's mine.'

'Oh, I'm not bothered about that.' Janetta smiled brilliantly and wrecked what was left of her face pack. 'That does it, I'll wash this lot off, then I think I'll take the dogs for a walk. I know you've just brought them back, Felice, but I could do with the exercise.'

'What a restless lot you are,' Serena grumbled, as Janetta left the kitchen and ran noisily up the stairs. 'I suppose it will be bedlam here tonight when we're all preparing for the dance. How are you getting there, by the way?'

'Charles is taking us. I expect he'll drive his estate so they'll be room for you as well, if you like.'

'Thanks, but I'd rather take myself than be a crushed sixth. I could phone an old boyfriend, of course, but then I'll have the hassle of ditching him when Tobias arrives. No, I'll definitely be best off on my own.'

'What if Tobias doesn't go?' Felice asked quietly.

'He will,' Serena replied with a confidence that twisted like a knife in Felice's aching heart.

She wasn't looking forward to the dance at all, but, when they were all dressed and ready that evening, she was conscious of a certain pride as she checked over her brothers and sister.

Garth and Gavin looked youthfully handsome in their dark suits and immaculate white shirts, their ties knotted neatly for once by her skilful fingers. Janetta was a vision in the floating pink chiffon, with her fair hair a riot of curls and her make-up so light that she looked angelically lovely.

Felice herself, swishing the billowing skirt of her blue silk gown into place, felt unaccustomedly feminine. The gown might not be new, but its scooped neckline revealed the swell of her breasts, and the fitted bodice flattered her neat waist. Blue eyeshadow and dark mascara emphasised her brilliant eyes, pink lipstick glossed her full lips and her fair hair fell luxuriantly to her shoulders.

She tried very hard to convince herself that she hadn't chosen the gown against a newer one because Tobias had once said blue suited her...

She glanced at Serena, exquisite in a figure-hugging black crêpe gown, with real diamonds gleaming at her ears and her fair hair secured elegantly above her graceful neck with diamond clips. Her make-up was vividly and professionally applied. She was so secure in her conviction that she was unmatchable that she didn't mind

Janetta looking stunning in the pink chiffon she'd lost interest in herself.

'There's a car,' Janetta said excitedly, as they all waited in the sitting-room, the girls drinking sherry and the boys settling for Coke.

'For heaven's sake don't peek through the curtains like that. It's only Charles,' Serena scolded, although she posed automatically as Gavin went to let him in.

Charles, immaculate in a dinner suit, looked admiringly at the three girls when he came in and exclaimed, 'Talk about being spoilt for choice. I didn't know you were coming with us as well, Serena, but we can make room.'

'Thanks, but I prefer to drive myself,' she replied, picking up her black crêpe evening bag and scarlet wrap, and using her model's walk to lead the way out of the room.

'She's a hard act to follow but we're no slouches ourselves,' Janetta whispered irrepressibly to Felice as they followed her out.

'For heaven's sake don't let Charles know Tobias might be attending or he won't talk about anything else all night,' Felice whispered back desperately. 'Charles is so ambitious his night will be ruined if Tobias doesn't turn up.'

And mine will be if he does, she added silently to herself, not knowing how she would be able to endure seeing Serena in Tobias's arms. It was a spectre that failed to materialise during the first couple of hours of the dance, when her undeniable popularity provided her with so many partners that she had no time to stand around brooding.

Brood she did, though, whoever's arms she happened to be in. The clubhouse was full to bursting, she knew just about everybody, and yet still she couldn't relax and enjoy herself as much as she usually did. All the time she kept wondering, waiting, and dreading that Tobias would put in an appearance. Her eyes kept straying to the door, and then to Serena, who was also watching for him.

She must be getting impatient, Felice thought. The evening was wearing away. It would be a blow to Serena's self-esteem if Tobias failed to appear—and a blow to her own heart if he did. She sighed, and the sound came from so deep within her that it almost hurt. Well, why not? Ever since she'd tumbled headlong in love with him she hadn't had a comfortable minute.

She was dancing with Charles at the time and he said indignantly, 'What was that sigh for?'

Felice felt so guilty because he was being particularly attentive tonight that she raised her hand to touch his cheek in a light gesture of apology. 'Sorry, my mind was wandering,' she confessed.

'That's not very flattering,' he complained, catching her hand and planting a cheeky kiss on her fingers.

At that moment the music ended, and a force Felice couldn't resist drew her eyes once more to the door. This time she knew he would be there, and he was.

Tobias.

He stood just inside the entrance, darkly handsome in a dinner suit and gleaming white shirt, his unruly hair tumbling across his forehead in such a heart-tuggingly familiar way that Felice's fingers itched to brush it back. The sudden pounding of her heart was familiar, too, and so was the stormy look in his dark eyes as he looked directly at her.

She frowned, bewildered, as he was always bewildering her. What was it to him if Charles's lips were still lingering on her fingers? She was thankful, though, when Charles lowered her hand and whirled her away as another dance began, so that Tobias was lost to her sight.

That was the last dance before the auction. Everybody drifted to their tables around the dance-floor and Charles escorted her to the Lawson table. They were the last to be seated, and Felice's heart fluttered like a wild thing when she saw that the chair next to Serena's was empty.

Her eyes went questioningly to Serena, who smiled and said, 'Tobias has arrived. He was cornered by some club officials in the bar but he'll join us any moment.'

'Tobias?' Charles exclaimed. 'You don't mean Tobias Hunter?'

'Who else?' Serena asked sweetly, and transferred her attention to the stage as a roll of drums brought all conversation to a halt.

The club chairman adjusted the microphone, then said into it, 'As you all know, this dance is the first of many functions we hold each year to raise money for charity. Our particular project this year is a recreation centre for handicapped children. We've set our sights on donating twenty thousand pounds—yes, I know that's a lot of money but, with fêtes, jumble sales and sponsored walks to come, I'm sure we can manage it. The profits from this function will start the ball rolling, boosted of course by the proceeds from our popular supper dance auction. So if all you gentlemen will get your cheque books ready, I'd like the ladies who have sportingly agreed to participate to stand up for a round of applause, please.'

Felice stood up with Janetta, Serena, and several other girls. They all gave a general wave round the ballroom and sat down again. In a friendly atmosphere like this there was no embarrassment because there was always somebody to bid, even for the plainest girls.

At least, there never had been any embarrassment before, but Felice was always self-conscious when Tobias was near. She was also acutely aware that Serena was looking round for him, and was hard put not to look for him herself.

'Thank you, ladies,' the club chairman went on. 'We'll proceed in alphabetical order as usual.' He called out a girl's name and the bidding began. The average sum reached was around twenty pounds but when Janetta's turn came the bidding was fiercer and Tom finally secured her for fifty pounds.

Felice whispered her congratulations but Janetta laughingly murmured, 'It's the pink chiffon. I wonder if I can coax Serena into making it a permanent loan?'

They both looked across the table at Serena, but she was looking over her shoulder towards the bar. Felice could have said what she was thinking for her: *Where* is Tobias? But then Felice's own name was called out and she pinned a smile on her face and tried to look like a good sport.

'What am I bid for this lovely and popular lady?' the chairman asked.

From the entrance to the bar, a deep Canadian voice drawled, 'Twenty thousand pounds.'

CHAPTER TWELVE

THERE was a stunned silence, then everybody's heads turned in disbelief towards Tobias. He was leaning nonchalantly against the door-frame of the bar, a drink in his hand, completely unruffled by the sensation he had caused.

Twenty thousand pounds! Felice just couldn't absorb the shock. The colour drained from her face and she was robbed of all power to move, speak or even think.

Her first wild reaction was that he was joking, and yet she knew he wasn't. His compelling eyes were riveted on her, making love to her, blatantly claiming her, as though she were the only person in the crowded ballroom who mattered. Or the only person there at all.

Felice was devastated. All right, so twenty thousand pounds might mean as little to him as fifty pounds meant to other people, but she'd never live down the sensation he'd caused. Never!

How could he single her out like this? How could he make her such a target for gossip? Now everybody would be whispering about her, conjecturing, and coming to the conclusion that she was so much more to him than his housekeeper.

Was this his way of punishing her for refusing to be his mistress, or was he manoeuvring her into a position where she might as well be, since after tonight everybody would think that she was, anyway? Whatever, Tobias was getting his precious entertainment value out of her now, and she hated him for it. Hated him!

The stunned silence still held and her eyes were still locked on to his as colour flooded back to her ashen cheeks with a vengeance. She blushed a fiery, guilty red, and it wasn't fair. She wasn't guilty of anything. She wasn't!

Serena, sitting like marble on the opposite side of the table, was the first to come out of shock. She said bitterly and distinctly, 'You devious bitch!'

Felice swallowed but no words came. Suddenly pandemonium broke loose as everybody started speaking at once. The babble increased until the club chairman used the microphone to call for order. As the noise died down, he said, 'That most amazingly generous offer meets our charity target in one go. I don't anticipate it will be surpassed, so the supper dance with Felice goes to our newest member, Mr Tobias Hunter.'

Charles, sitting stunned beside her, came to his senses enough to gasp, 'What's going on between you two?'

Felice scarcely heard him. She was watching Tobias walking purposefully towards her, threading his way around the tables, coming inexorably closer and closer. Her nerve broke and she got up and fled, causing an even bigger sensation than his incredible bid.

Dimly she was aware that the twins, Tom and Charles were rising, too, but she heard Janetta order sharply, 'Leave them alone! It's a lovers' tiff, that's all.'

She'd spoken loud enough for half the hall to hear and Felice thought, 'That's all?' With Tobias changing direction to come after her, what did it need to be really something?

She fled out of the hall and into the car park. Only then did it occur to her that she hadn't brought her own car. The clubhouse was out in the country and she couldn't get away without transport. She would have to go in again and phone for a taxi.

She turned, but there was Tobias so close behind that she turned again, lifted her full skirts and ran in the opposite direction. She didn't get far before Tobias caught up with her and snatched her up in his arms.

She struggled and kicked but his arms only tightened as he carried her to his Jaguar and dumped her unceremoniously inside. 'Stay there or I'll strip off that gown so you can't run away,' he threatened.

'You wouldn't dare!' she panted.

'You know I would. I've bought your company for the supper dance—shall we say an hour of your precious time? I mean to have every minute of it, so you can make it easy on yourself or you can make it hard. Which is it to be?'

'I hate you,' Felice said. 'You've ruined my life. You've made everybody talk about me. Even Serena called me a devious bitch.'

'She's the devious bitch,' he said shortly, pushing the billowing folds of her skirt inside the car door and slamming it shut. Then he was beside her, overwhelming her as he always did by the force and power of his presence.

She shrank back into her seat as he leaned over to pull her seat belt across her and snap it into place. His purposeful hands brushed her breasts and she quivered with far more than anger, hating both herself and him for her reaction.

Her mind was having trouble keeping up with the physical sensations that flooded her, partly because she was still coming to terms with being manhandled as easily as if she had as little substance as a rag doll.

She wasn't used to being defenceless, and yet that was exactly how she felt when the powerful engine roared to life and the headlights snapped on. Almost mesmerised, she watched them probe ahead as Tobias drove out of the car park and gunned the car expertly along the narrow lanes.

For several minutes Felice fought to maintain a dignified silence while Tobias drove on through the night. Finally her overwrought emotions got the better of her and she burst out, 'Twenty thousand pounds! How *could* you? I have to live here, you know. I can't go swanning off to Canada when things get tough. Now everybody will think I'm a whore.'

'If you were a whore you wouldn't be here now, and neither would I. It wouldn't be necessary,' he replied grimly.

'What am I supposed to make of that?' she demanded.

'You're supposed to stop being silly. Nobody will think any the worse of you, and if they do, it's their problem. The next time they see you again you will be my wife.'

Felice failed to see the joke and said bitterly, 'I'll give you ten out of ten for a sense of humour.'

'I was never more serious in my life.'

'Then you must be crazy.'

'Yes,' Tobias agreed calmly. 'Crazy about you.'

Felice couldn't accept that and she cried, 'Crazy to get me to bed with you, perhaps.'

'That, too,' he agreed.

'What do you mean, "That, too"? That's all it is. All it's ever been with you. This is all spite because I wouldn't become one of your mistresses. You're so used to winning you simply can't bear to lose!'

'I certainly couldn't bear to lose you.'

It was driving her mad, the way he kept agreeing with her, and yet not agreeing with her, and she exploded, 'You mean your ego couldn't bear to lose! And because of that, you've deliberately humiliated me, made everybody think—think——'

Words failed her, and Tobias broke in savagely, 'If anybody is going to be humiliated tonight, it's going to be me. That's my problem, and to hell with everybody else, including Serena. Just get it through that lovely head of yours that I'm the only one you have to worry about tonight.'

Lovely head...? Having made her the subject of every spiteful tongue in the district, manhandled and kidnapped her, was he now trying to *charm* her into bed? Well, he'd left it a bit late! Felice opened her mouth to tell him so, when the car slowed and she demanded in alarm, 'Why are we stopping?'

'We're home. Our home—Woodlands. Or it will be as soon as we're married.'

'It's not my home,' she snapped, unable to believe that even Tobias would stoop to such deception to get his own way. 'Even if you were serious, I'd never marry you.'

'I warned you once before not to say "never" to me,' he reminded her calmly as he released her seatbelt, 'but I'm willing to let that pass for the moment. I'm sorry I've had to be so rough with you, but you gave me little choice. It was the only way I could get your attention for more than five minutes at a time. I'll explain everything when we're inside.'

'No!' she exclaimed, distrusting him.

'Yes,' he contradicted. 'You can tell me all your reasons why you're not going to marry me, then I'll tell you my reasons why you are.' He looked at the clock on the dashboard and added, 'I still have forty-five minutes of your time. Of course, if you prefer to stay here...'

He leaned towards her and Felice got hastily out of the car. The joke, when he finally sprung it, was bound to catch her unawares, and she didn't want to be within arm's reach of him at the time. Shivering in the cold night air and shaking out the crushed folds of her gown, she followed him into the Hall and through to the library.

He indicated an armchair by the fire. She sat down reluctantly, watching him like a hawk as he added logs to the glowing embers of the fire. He studied the logs as the embers kindled to flame, then turned to her with a crooked smile that tugged at her heart-strings.

'No woodlice for you to save tonight, Felice,' he said softly. 'Only me—from my loneliness. Will that loving heart of yours stretch to take me on as well?'

'Stop it! Stop playing with me,' she flared, jumping out of the armchair and prowling restlessly around the room. 'You've had your fun. Let me go home now.'

'You are home,' he told her. 'Sometimes I'll have to take you away from it because I want you with me wherever I go, but I'll bring you back often enough to keep you happy. I promise——'

'Stop it!' Felice cried again, her hands clenching into fists at what she saw as his merciless determination to play out to the bitter end the game he was making of her. 'Just stop it.'

'But I can't,' he replied, his voice deepening in the way that had bewitched and bewildered her over the past traumatic weeks. 'Tonight has always been inevitable, Felice. We've both fought against it for different reasons, but we've both been wasting our time. I've known it for a long time now. Haven't you?'

'No!' she exclaimed, incensed. 'All I know is that I've been preparing this house for your mistress, the one you picked out to have your children. Have you forgotten about her?'

'Not for a moment,' Tobias replied, coming towards her. 'She haunts me day and night, wrecking my sleep, driving me to distraction. Housekeeper, mistress, wife—they've always been one person in my mind. You, Felice.'

'I don't believe you,' she whispered, her voice almost breaking on a sob.

'It's the truth,' Tobias told her, coming closer still. 'You love Woodlands so much—how could I possibly let anybody else loose on it? You've been preparing this house for yourself, my darling. I haven't been able to tell you until now because you had too many things against me.'

Felice's heart began to pound, but she was still frightened to trust the message it was pulsing to every taut nerve in her body. 'What was Serena, then?' she asked desperately. 'A convenient diversion?'

'Serena was a mistake, and you can blame yourself for that. All I've had of your company were whatever crumbs you cared to throw my way while you were working for me. It wasn't enough and it will never be enough. You chose to spend your spare time with somebody else, and I refuse to be responsible for the things I do when I'm out of my mind with jealousy. Stop making me jealous, and there won't be any more Serenas in my life. I won't need them.'

Felice caught her breath, and as she felt a betraying surge of tears, she blinked furiously and begged, 'Stop playing with me, Tobias. You've had your fun...your revenge. Let me go. Please...'

'That's the one thing I can't do, my darling. I love you far too much.'

Felice's white teeth bit hard into her full lower lip, and she protested, 'If you loved me, if you knew even *any* small thing about love, you wouldn't have made that dreadful bid for me at the auction.'

Tobias was so close by now he towered over her. He took her trembling hands in his, sapping what little resistance to him she had left. His voice throbbed as he breathed, 'That wasn't a bid, it was a declaration of love. Everybody knew it except you, my woolly-headed little darling.'

'D-don't call me that,' Felice stuttered, starting to panic now that she had no fury left to sustain her. 'I'm not your darling!'

'Yes, you are.'

'Don't!' she insisted, adding foolishly, 'I'm certainly not little, anyway.'

'No, my darling, you are the most stunning of the lovely Lawson girls. The pick of the batch. Not only stunning but kind, caring and loving. How many girls would throw away their own ambitions to raise their younger brothers and sister, and make such a fine job of it? Just the sort of job I know you'll do on our children.'

'Stop it!' Felice begged desperately. 'If you've been listening to Janetta and the boys, they're biased and——'

'I've been listening to my own heart,' he broke in. 'If I'd listened to it in the first place none of this would have happened. Unfortunately, your kind of integrity, love and loyalty is too rare for a man like me to believe in right away. Can you forgive me for my doubts, Felice? Doubts I learned from others but punished you for?'

'I can't believe you're saying all this,' she whispered, her heart breaking with love for this humble man who was so different from the stormy Tobias who'd made her life both heaven and hell. He sounded as though he had a heart that could feel love and pain in the same way hers could.

'I'm saying it, and I'll keep on saying it until you believe me.'

'Oh, don't,' she begged again.

'What do you mean—don't?' Tobias asked, his patience wearing thin and his dark eyebrows snapping together in the way she knew so well.

'I mean you don't have to explain anything to me. Not if——' She wanted to say 'not if you truly love me' but the words wouldn't come. She still felt too insecure, too shy.

'I do have to explain otherwise you'll never understand why I was so suspicious of you.' Tobias lifted her hands to his lips and kissed them lingeringly before he continued, 'Twelve years ago I married a woman who didn't want me, but the things I could give her. A gold-digger, in fact, although I couldn't see it at the time. When I did, it cost me a lot of wrangling, a lot of bitterness and a fortune to get rid of her.'

He smiled, but it was a smile made painful by bitter self-mockery. 'I thought that in the long run the experience was worth it because it made me too smart ever to be caught a second time. I vowed I'd never again confuse wanting a woman with loving her, and I didn't. Whenever I fancied a woman after that, I paid first and walked away a free man before disillusion could set in. It worked like a charm until I met you, Felice.'

He took her face gently between his strong hands, staring intently into her eyes. 'I fell for you within

minutes of meeting you, but I was too cynical to believe
it was love. By the time I realised you were as loving as
you were lovely, as genuine as you were loyal, it was too
late. I'd spoilt it all.'

He sighed and kissed her hair gently, then pulled her
against him and cradled her head into his shoulder. Felice
felt the warmth and strength of his hard body. It no
longer seemed a threat but a power she could depend
upon. She knew she was being overwhelmed again,
trapped, and yet it was in such a delicious way...

After a moment, Tobias continued, 'Deep inside I
always knew you were really as wonderful as you appeared to be—but I needed to doubt. To protect myself,
I punished you. I drove you away from me, and you
kept on running, no matter how hard I chased.'

He turned her face up to his and pleaded, 'Don't run
any more, my darling. I've been going out of my mind
with jealousy and despair.'

'You?' she whispered wonderingly.

'Yes, me. That red-headed fellow who was drooling
all over you in the village this morning and at the dance
this evening will never know how close he came to being
flattened.'

'He's just a friend, Tobias.'

'That's more than I am, isn't it?' he asked bitterly.

Felice saw all the anguish she'd been suffering herself
reflected in his face. Her heart lurched, and she asked
with difficulty, 'If—if you felt like this about me, why
did you date Serena?'

'Because you wouldn't come out with me. Because I
was out of my mind with jealousy. Because—oh, my
God, Felice, don't you realise I haven't said or done a
rational thing since I first met you?'

That struck a chord Felice couldn't doubt, so aptly did it describe the way she'd been feeling and behaving herself, and yet there were still things she needed to know. 'It didn't seem too rational the way you chased me in your car this morning,' she admitted. 'I still don't know why you did.'

'I'd reached the end of my tether. I was going to risk telling you that I loved you.'

'Risk?' she echoed, bewildered.

'Yes, risk. I'd made you despise me so much that I only had your love for Woodlands to work on to keep you close to me. I hoped that in time you'd forgive me for all the mistakes I'd made and give me a second chance. But all you were interested in was the house, never me. You didn't give me any opportunity to get closer to you, and I couldn't show how I really felt about you. With my track record, you'd have thought I was only trying to get you into bed with me, and I was frightened you'd take off for good.'

The thought of Tobias being frightened was something Felice was still trying to get to grips with when he said, 'I gambled everything on tonight, and I still don't know whether I've won or lost.'

Felice stirred in his arms, and raised her head from his shoulder to look up into his eyes. 'What if you've lost?' she asked.

Tobias's face hardened. 'Then I'll try something else, and keep on trying until you give up. One thing you'd better understand, and understand right now, is that *I'm* never going to give up.'

That sounded more like the Tobias she knew—and loved to the point of madness. But she still had enough spirit left to object, 'That sounds more like an ultimatum than a proposal of marriage.'

'It's the way I feel,' he growled.

'Because you think I'm suitable for bearing your children?'

Tobias grasped her shoulders and shook her none too gently. 'I no longer care if we don't have any. I *love* you, can't you understand that? I can't even *look* at another woman.'

A brief flare of jealousy made Felice grumble, 'Serena would have something to say about that.'

'I never looked at Serena, not in the way I look at you. I endured her company because I couldn't have yours. You can blame yourself for that.'

'Somehow I knew it would come round to being all my fault,' Felice murmured. 'I suppose if our marriage doesn't work, that will be my fault as well.'

Tobias realised what she'd said before she did herself. His arms tightened around her and he buried his face in her hair. 'Then you will marry me? Oh, my love, you'll never regret it, and our marriage will work. The way I love you, it can't fail.' He lifted his head to gaze at her, and added, 'So long as you love me, too. Tell me that you do, my darling.'

The uncertainty in his eyes went straight to Felice's heart, banishing the last of her doubts. 'I love you,' she admitted at last, and sighed as though a burden had fallen from her. 'So very, very much.'

She heard Tobias sigh as well, and knew he was feeling the same kind of release that had freed her of the unhappiness of the past few weeks. His lips closed on hers, claiming all the love she'd withheld so stubbornly from him, and giving in return all the love that he was capable of.

It was more than enough. So profound was the emotion flowing between them that the world receded until only they had any reality.

When Tobias raised his head again, it was only by a fraction so that he could murmur against her lips, 'We'll fly to London tomorrow and be married by special licence as soon as we can. We can have a proper wedding here later if you like, but I must and will make you my wife as soon as possible.'

Felice drew away from him a fraction more to ask teasingly, 'So I don't get any time to change my mind?'

'No, you don't,' he replied, passion roughening his voice. 'No time at all. You have to trust yourself to me. I know we've fought, but I'll spend the rest of my life making up for it.'

'Oh, Tobias,' she sighed, winding her arms around his neck and brushing her lips against his provocatively, 'I wouldn't have missed a moment of it, beast that you are.'

'Tame me,' he breathed, and kissed her.

'Tame me,' she responded, and kissed him back.

But the bonding of their lips inflamed them both. It fired all the passion that had been simmering beneath the surface since their eyes first met, their hands first touched and they first learned the danger of being in each other's arms.

Tobias groaned, thrust her away from him, and said between clenched teeth, 'I'm not quite—civilised right now. You'd better take yourself off to one of the bedrooms, right this moment, while you still can. I don't want you thinking I've brought you here just to seduce you.'

Felice stretched out a hand to touch his stormy face with loving fingers. She sighed, thinking that a nice girl

would flee this very instant. But she stayed and asked
tremulously, 'What if I want to be seduced?'

'For God's sake, don't torment me now, Felice! I'm
trying to do things right for once in my life.'

'So am I,' she responded, 'and I can't see how you
and I staying together, feeling the way we do about each
other, can possibly be wrong.'

Once more she was given no chance to reconsider.
Tobias swept her up in his arms and strode with her to
the couch by the fire, sitting down with her still in his
arms. She coiled her arms around his neck and drew his
dark head down to hers, scattering kisses all over his
face, and receiving his in return.

She felt his hand slide from her neck to her shoulder,
and gasped as it slid under the silk of her ballgown to
cup her breast. Her nipple tautened, demanding his attention, and she gasped as his probing fingers found and
grasped it.

Sensations so sweet suffused Felice's entire body that
she could scarcely breathe for a moment. She went limp
in his arms, her head falling back so that he could press
burning kisses along the supple line of her throat.

She didn't feel him unzip the back of her bodice, but
she felt the soft silk slip from her shoulders, exposing
both her breasts to him. He bent his head and kissed
them lingeringly in turn, his lips fastening against first
one nipple and then the other.

'My lovely Felice,' he murmured. 'My magnificent
darling.'

For the first time in her life she felt not too much of
a woman, but just enough, and a surge of passion banished her weakness and gave her a power of her own.

She unbuttoned his dinner-jacket and then his shirt,
and threw them aside as he shrugged out of them. They

were both bare to the waist now, and flesh called to flesh, so that he once more clasped her against him.

They both gasped as her soft breasts were clamped against the hard hairiness of his chest, neither moving for long moments until their lips instinctively bonded again. Still kissing her, Tobias lifted her up and laid her gently on the fur rug in front of the log fire.

Vaguely Felice remembered how jealous she'd been when she'd thought of Tobias claiming a woman right here, and in this passionate way. She'd always wanted to be that woman and, even now, she could scarcely believe that she was.

It was almost dreamlike, but then Tobias began to take off the rest of her clothes, kissing every inch of newly exposed flesh, and her responses became earthy, primitive, very much of this world.

His own clothes became a hindrance and she stripped them off him, her hands running possessively over the lean length of him, glorying in his strength and the latent power she detected under his rippling muscles.

'I love you,' he murmured, kissing his way from her breasts to her midriff, then his tongue reaching and exploring her navel. As he continued his downward quest, he demanded roughly, 'Say you love me, too. Say it, Felice.'

'I love you,' she whispered, her hands exploring the taut muscles of his shoulders and back. 'You'll never know how much.'

'I need to know now,' he gasped, kissing her silken thighs as he parted them.

'I love you,' she repeated, and then her body arched in an explosion of sensation as he discovered and explored the secret parts of her. 'Tobias,' she added brokenly. 'Tobias, for heaven's sake...'

But he had reached the limit of his own endurance and he thrust into her, uniting them in the flames of passion that had been threatening to consume them for so long. Felice, responding to his frantic demands for satisfaction and matching it with demands of her own, knew that her senses hadn't played her false. This was the ultimate consummation, the ultimate act of a love that both had craved but resisted for so long.

When Tobias collapsed against her with a great cry, she cradled him to her, keeping him safe until strength and reason returned to both of them. This was her moment, she thought, her eyes misty with tears. He was totally hers now. And she was totally his.

She felt complete, sated, no tiny corner of her questioning or unloved. When Tobias finally moved away and cradled her, in his turn, in his arms, she lay against him, the happiest woman in the world.

When he spoke at last, it was to ask, 'Are you warm enough?'

'Mmm...' she replied dreamily.

He still reached up, snatched a rug from the couch and spread it over them before he lay down again. 'No regrets?' he asked anxiously, flooding her again with the need to soothe and reassure him.

'What regrets should I have?' she teased. 'You're not going to spank me on the bottom and send me back to the servants' quarters, are you?'

Tobias laughed and hugged her. 'You sound like yourself again. The lovely, laughing girl who met me from the plane when I first came to Woodlands... the girl I was so harsh with... the girl I've been pining for ever since. I was so afraid I'd killed off all that was best in you.'

Felice pressed her face into his shoulder and murmured, 'You got what you wanted in the end, though, didn't you? I've ended up what I was determined not to be—your mistress.'

Tobias tangled his hand in her hair and pulled her face away from his shoulder so that she had to meet his eyes. 'Don't say that,' he growled. 'We'll be married in a few days.'

Felice smiled at him. 'It's not so important any more. Now that I know I'm loved, the ring doesn't seem to matter.'

'It matters to me,' Tobias responded fiercely, his hand tightening in her hair. 'I won't rest until you're tied to me so tightly you'll never get free.'

'I thought that was your own particular nightmare— never getting free, I mean.'

Tobias began to kiss the strands of her hair that were twined like silk between his fingers. 'That was before I knew what it was like to love a woman I had no claim on at all. It was hell. Why do you think I couldn't stay away from Woodlands? Why do you think I found a way to tie you to Woodlands? Why do you think I stopped you working as a taxi driver?'

'Tell me,' she invited, entranced by this lover-like side of Tobias that had been hidden from her for so long.

'To keep you close, to keep you safe, until I could claim you for my own. But you kept wriggling free. This time you won't, though,' he vowed, releasing her hair and pushing her head back to the safety of his shoulder.

Felice kissed his salty skin and confessed, 'I've loved you since day one, but I wouldn't admit it even to myself. I'm still not sure why you didn't fall for Serena—or even Janetta. They're both so much lovelier than I am.'

'In a standard sort of way, perhaps, but I've never been interested in what was standard. I'm a high-flyer, Felice, and nothing less than exceptional satisfies me. You, my magnificent darling.'

She felt her eyes moisten with tears again, and said huskily, 'I'm beginning to think you really do love me.'

'Beginning to think...?' he questioned, almost speechlessly. 'Do you think I'd be prepared to live in this mausoleum of a house if it wasn't for love of you?'

'It isn't a mausoleum,' Felice objected, her head snapping up indignantly. 'It's a beautiful house.'

'It's a folly,' he replied in a voice that brooked no argument. Then his voice softened and he continued, 'Maybe we should crack open a bottle of champagne and drink to folly. Is there any champagne in the house?'

'No,' Felice admitted forlornly, 'and I thought I was a pretty good housekeeper, too. I'll just have to try to be a better mistress.'

'A better *wife*,' Tobias corrected her severely. 'Well, if we can't drink to folly, what shall we do?'

'We could always make love,' she offered hopefully.

'Truly a girl after my own heart,' he breathed, and folded her into his arms again.

**THREE UNFORGETTABLE HEROINES
THREE AWARD-WINNING AUTHORS**

MAVERICK HEARTS

A unique collection of historical short stories that
capture the spirit of America's last frontier.

HEATHER GRAHAM POZZESSERE—over 10 million copies
of her books in print worldwide
Lonesome Rider—The story of an Eastern widow and the
renegade half-breed who becomes her protector.

PATRICIA POTTER—an author whose books are consistently
Waldenbooks bestsellers
Against the Wind—Two people, battered by heartache, prove
that love can heal all.

JOAN JOHNSTON—award-winning Western historical author
with 17 books to her credit
One Simple Wish—A woman with a past discovers that
dreams really do come true.

Join us for an exciting journey West with
UNTAMED
Available in July, wherever Harlequin books are sold.

MAV/93